I0686889

For the Love of Three

Cascade Bay, Volume 5

Solara Gordon

Published by THE EARTH MOVED, LLC, 2023.

FOR THE LOVE OF THREE

First edition. August 13, 2023.

ISBN: 979-8988654902

Written by Solara Gordon.

Also by Solara Gordon

Cascade Bay
Love Reborn
Reunited By Choice
Love's Triple Play
Three Hearts In Love
For the Love of Three

Cauldron Falls
Believe In Love
A Christmas Reunion

Peyton Corners
Falling for You
Caught by Love's Slow Burn

Standalone

A Heart's Desire
To Love You Again
To Love You Again

Watch for more at https://solaragordon.com/.

This is for the polyamorists amongst us. This is for my readers and my street team, Solara's Glamorous Stars. This is for all who enjoy a steamy spicy romance that takes you on a journey with the characters.

Thank you to my polyamory family. Thank you to my readers and street team, Solara's Glamorous Stars. You all inspire, encourage and ignite the sparks that create each and every story.

Keep the sparks going and igniting more stories and inspiration!

Solara Gordon

Chapter One

"I'm going to see about getting us rooms and find out when this storm might let up." Mason Cox glanced at his best friend, David Swanson and Joan Nelson. Mason handed David his flight brief and captain's cap.

"The line at the concierge is growing. I'll be back in a few moments." Mason moved forward, focusing on the message board just above the exit. A stalled storm with growing intensity and a rapidly dwindling list of places to stay wasn't helping his determination.

When Joan and David began dating, Mason had sworn his heart wasn't involved. *You can't lie to yourself any longer*, his conscience crowed. How much more could he keep in? If he lingered, his ebbing patience might be gone. Probably best to put some space between them for now and work on regaining his self-control while he checked on getting them accommodations.

Getting caught by the impeding storm rubbed his limited tolerance up against his tired, frayed nerves. What he'd give to be home after a hot meal and shower in his recliner, reading the mystery he'd forgotten to pack two days prior!

He stopped halfway to the counter and glanced over his shoulder, watching David move closer to Joan. Prior to Joan dating David, the three of them spent time together. Not any exclusivity. Just three friends enjoying hanging out. What if the three of them had to share a room?

Mason held his breath and reminded himself why he and David were best friends. Being two tall, geeky-looking teens ostracized by the popular crowd for being different cemented their bond in high school. College and career goals had separated them until a chance reunion

occurred thanks to a mutual acquaintance. Who knew their keen interest in model planes and aerodynamics would reunite them far from their Midwestern roots?

David watched Mason stalk away. Joan's weak smile punched David in the gut. The two people he cared for the most appeared to be at odds. He didn't get it. Every time he'd asked Mason about dating Joan, Mason had said he was okay with it.

David tugged Joan into his embrace. "Hon, I know it's not what you expected. None of us did. The storm came up faster than predicted."

Joan nuzzled his neck and hugged him back. Her spicy perfume filled his nostrils. His cock nudged his fly as images of her dabbing the scent between her bare breasts and along her neck filled his mind. Her lithe build and sensual curves nestled against him in all the right spots. Except the middle of the employee lounge wasn't the correct place.

David stepped back, putting space between them. He cupped her cheek and looked into her blue eyes. Threading his fingers into her short auburn hair, he brushed his lips against hers.

David wanted to reassure Joan, and at the same time, he wanted to grab Mason to get to the bottom of what had him pissed off. "Let's find Mason and see what's going on. I'm sure once we know more, things won't look so bad."

Joan's subdued nod tugged at David's heart. He'd been in love with her ever since he and Mason moved in two doors down from her in Cascade Bay. A quirk of fate and the Pacific Northwest gaining another NASA contract had landed them jobs with a local medium-sized airline headquartered in San Francisco.

Flying standby to get back to San Francisco wasn't easy. Cramped flights full of folks trying to beat the freak storm bearing down on the Pacific Northwest had bumped them to another flight. The approaching snowstorm grounded their flight's last leg after landing in Spokane.

Joan followed in David's wake. His warm hand held hers, but it didn't comfort her. She'd seen the look on Mason's face as the message board updated with more flight cancellations. Ever since she started going out with David, Mason had pulled away. It was almost like he walled himself off. She missed their mutual laughs and spontaneous hugs.

Sex with David was great. She wondered what it would be like with Mason. Or even both at the same time. She'd overheard stories about them sharing other women and threesomes. No one seemed to complain. What kind of reaction would she get if she mentioned her fantasy?

Mason rushed toward them, frowning, his brow furled. He looked like he could use a hug and some friendly snuggles. She missed their Friday night puppy piles in front of her plasma TV, watching old movies and munching popcorn until midnight. Why did he keep turning her down?

"I got us the last room available, a king bed and kitchenette." His determined stare took on a fierce quality when he sighed.

Joan reached out with her free hand, wanting to take his hand and reassure him. His presence, along with David's, settled her anxious heart. Being with them, she felt safe. Mason's quick wit and questioning mind pushed her to grow and learn. David's sweet nature and boyish charms nurtured her softer side. If a man existed with both their strengths and attractiveness, she hadn't found him. She really had the best situation, both of them caring for her.

"Why are you scowling?" David asked, squeezing Joan's hand. "It isn't like we don't know each other."

"One bed and three of us..." Mason's voice trailed off.

A huge lump threatened to constrict his throat. Couldn't they stop touching? He hated feeling alone and outside like a third wheel upsetting the balance. He'd nearly taken Joan's hand when she reached toward him. How long did he keep his feelings silent? Jealousy wasn't an issue. Or was it? He hated being prickly about it.

"I say we deal with it as best we can and go from there," Joan offered. "I'm tired and hungry. What about you?"

She interlaced her fingers with his. Warmth spiraled up his arm and straight into the pit of his stomach. Her soft skin and scent drove him to distraction. He noticed her slight smile as she held both their hands. Had she winked at him? Stuck her tongue out and licked her lips as she winked? What was she up to?

David shrugged and wrapped his arm around Joan's waist. Was David aware of Joan's actions?

Mason swallowed hard and forced himself to breathe deeper. His pulse refused to slow down each time her fingers brushed over his wrist. He didn't think he could withstand much more without pulling his hand away.

David's arched eyebrow caught him off guard. Crap, he knew! He had to know! Mason began to pull his hand free from Joan's. Mason started to shake his head no when David smiled at him. Confusion flared, and an uneasy feeling crept into his stomach. Something was up, and he didn't know what.

How could Joan be content holding hands with both of them? Was she playing them against each other? Anxiety inched up his back and fueled the acid lapping higher in his throat.

"What did they say about the storm?" David's question threw him off guard. Why the change of subject?

"There's a break right now. Planes can't get out due to the low ceiling level. Folks are making a run for food and needed items. One of the baggage handlers is going to the local Walmart. We can ride along."

"What about our luggage?" Joan asked, refusing to let go of his hand.

"I found it and sent it ahead to the room. Reports are this storm could last three or four days. We've got a change of clothes apiece." Mason wondered if the implications of sharing a room, much less the same bed, conjured similar images for David and Joan as those running through his mind.

"I could use a couple of books and some food to keep me occupied over the next few days. Maybe a couple extra changes of clothes." David winked at him and slid him a sideways grin.

Mason gulped. He'd seen that signal before. The last time David used that signal, they'd brought the Yancy twins and two boxes of condoms home. David had an idea brewing.

At the hotel

Joan stomped her feet, knocking snow off her shoes. The room's outside entrance forced them through the ankle-deep accumulation covering the parking lot.

Mason's voice carried over the wind whistling up the open stairwell. "Thanks for the ride. If we need anything, we'll let you know."

A car door slammed, followed by another. Rustling of bags and David's "damn" reverberated up the stairs. She couldn't help grinning. Had he misjudged the powdery flakes like she had?

Pulling the room key from her coat pocket, she unlocked the door. Darkness greeted her. She fumbled along the closest wall until she found a light switch. A bedside table lamp glowed warmly. Blinking, she inhaled sharply. Three days in tight quarters? Joan moved further into the room.

Footsteps echoed up the steps and through the open door. Mason and David's laughter grew louder with their approach. Joan dropped her bags on the bed and went to help them.

Mason entered first. His six-foot height matched hers in heels. Snowflakes melted against his rich brown hair. He thrust his bag-filled hands at her. "David's got the rest up to his elbows. I'll be back in a minute."

Shaking her head, she placed the bags on the foot of the bed. Dare she peek inside? Both refused to check out with her and kept looking at each other with smug smiles. They'd taken quite a few minutes talking in the men's toiletries aisle. She'd overheard lubricated versus unlubricated. Then one of them headed to the pharmacy, claiming they needed aspirin.

Curiosity almost got the better of her. David's *whoosh* interrupted her. He rushed in, shaking his head and red hair, sprinkling her with the wet spray. Mason was right behind him, peering over his shoulder.

"Hey, do you mind?" She grinned at the two of them. Somehow the image of her sandwiched between David and Mason flared in her mind. What could a group hug hurt?

She moved forward and snaked her arms around David's waist. Pressing tight against him, she slid her arms past his back, reaching for Mason. Instead, she encountered plastic bags. Her partly closed eyes flew open, meeting Mason's quizzical gawk. He nibbled his lip as though he stopped himself from commenting. Again, he was holding back. Why? She didn't get it. His aloofness was beginning to bother her. The anxiousness pricking of her conscience sent chilled tendrils coursing down her back.

David's "hmmm, warmth" broke her musings. Mason's slight shake of his head prevented her from voicing her concerns. For now, she'd be quiet. Eventually, she'd get her questions answered.

"How about letting me all the way in so I can warm my backside?" Mason joked. "The wind is getting colder by the moment."

Joan took two bags from David and turned toward the small kitchenette at the back of the room. One-third of the countertop was taken up by the refrigerator, coffeemaker, and microwave. Another third contained a small sink. Setting the bags down on the remaining third, she opened one of the three available cabinets, discovering a hot plate and a variety of pans.

Surveying the contents of the other two, she located mugs, plates, glasses, and utensils.

Her earlier reaction to the room made her smirk. The size and compact arrangements didn't seem as tight. Off to the side, a table and three chairs pushed up against the partition separating the bedroom from the kitchenette. The bed faced the main doorway and single window.

Footsteps sounded behind her. Turning, she found Mason approaching her. He appeared more at ease. His prior stiff posture and hard glare were gone. She waited until he was very close. Leaning into him, she brushed her lips over his. He didn't pull away. Taking his packages, she whispered to him. "I don't know what's up, but please relax. I hate seeing you uptight."

Mason shrugged and began unpacking food and toiletry items.

David joined them, carrying their suitcases into the small closet. "There are a few hangers in here. Did either of you get anything that needs hanging up?"

"Our uniforms will use a couple. How many more do you need?" Joan moved to the bed and picked up her packages, counting the items needing immediate care. Rounding its corner, she stumbled over two bags. The contents spilled across the floor.

Chapter Two

Joan reached for the small box near her foot. David hurried over and began grabbing things, stuffing them into the open sack. "I can get it easier. You go ahead and hang up your stuff."

Nodding, she sidestepped and walked to the closet area. Mason's attempted indifference didn't get past her. He refused to look her in the eye. It served to confirm something was up. She'd only gotten a quick look at the box in David's hand, and part of the print was covered. If she read it correctly, sex and protection were in the mix. Warmth crept up her neck and cheeks, adding to the nervous energy pooling in her stomach.

Unpacking her suitcase, she hung her extra flight attendant uniform alongside her coat. What she needed was a long soak to take the chill out of her. With only a shower stall, she'd have to make do with a quick hot shower. Hopefully, there was enough hot water for the three of them.

At the rear of the closet, three shelves provided added storage. She placed her extra clothing and toiletries on one shelf. Her panties and bras looked out of place out in the open. Would the guys ignore them or remark about them? She loved color, especially soft pastels. There were no regulations on underwear colors, so she wore what she liked. Besides, David already knew this like she did about his white briefs and T-shirts.

Mason was another matter. He rushed past her, clutching a red cloth as he headed toward the bathroom.

"I get dibs on the shower," he called out, clicking the door shut.

"What's with you two and the looks at Walmart?" Joan shook her head and walked to the table where David sat, clipping price tags off his purchases.

"Nothing, hon. You know how guys talk." His grin set off an uneasy feeling. Their actions raised her anxiety level.

Rubbing her arms, Joan sat in the chair next to David. "I suppose I'm cooking. Unless one of you can do it without messing up everything and setting off the smoke detector."

"You know the extent of my culinary skills, and Mason's limited repertoire doesn't cover what we bought." David offered his hand. "Besides, you look like you could use a hug. What's bothering you?"

She could say nothing like him. Keep her uneasiness bottled up. Of course, it wouldn't help the butterflies and acid mix bubbling in her stomach. How much did she say without Mason present? Three days together in close quarters could make or break their friendship, along with her and David's relationship. Deciding the less said, the better, she leaned against him. "I'm just tired and hungry. And a bit worried about Mason. He seems stressed."

David slipped his arm around Joan's waist, snuggling her closer. "He's been working some strange hours. I imagine a few days off is what he needs."

David kissed Joan's cheek and hugged her. "Why don't you start dinner while I unpack Mason's and my stuff?"

"Only if I get to decide what we have." Joan's folded arms and intent expression made him swallow his cheeky retort. Three days with each of them in foul humor? No, that was unacceptable.

"How about this? We decide on a themed meal and open the wine we got."

David wished Mason had talked more while they were at Walmart. His cryptic answers left too many variables unknown. Mason agreed Joan was a hottie. That he liked her. But his less-than-enthusiastic discussion in the pharmacy area puzzled David. Time for clarification had come.

"Let me ask Mason what he wants hung up and grab a shower myself. I promise to leave you a few drops of water."

Rising, David grabbed his sleep shorts off the table and brushed his lips across hers. "Don't stress. It's gonna be okay."

Mason stripped off his light blue boxers. His semi-hard cock stuck out as though it accused him of being guilty. He didn't need more reminders of where his thoughts ran every time he looked at the box of condoms David had insisted on getting. The heated air from the overhead fan felt good, circulating along his aching shoulders and neck. Turning toward the shower, he saw his reflection in the full-length mirror on back of the bathroom door.

"Shit, I'd worry, too, if I saw someone scowling like that." He forced a smile to his lips. It looked just as ridiculous. What had him so tense?

His otherwise neat hair stood up in several places. How many times had he run his hands through it since entering the bathroom? The tired lines creasing his brow and the rigid set of his jaw didn't fool anyone. He was upset. Why? Getting that figured out would help him regain his composure.

Joan got him so hot and bothered. Pictures of her in her pajama shorts sprawled on the floor came to mind. Her soft kisses in between movies left him wanting to touch her and deepen the kiss. Hell, even the feel of her breasts crushed against his chest as she hugged the stuffing out

of him recently had struck a nerve he hadn't been aware of. Joan was the one. The woman he'd missed out on. Now she was with David. A guy didn't hit on his friend's lady.

Sliding his hands down his chest, Mason stopped at his waist. His back hurt from sitting in the cramped cockpit and stifling his emotions to the point of denial. Raising his right arm, he leaned to the left, stretching and pulling his cramped muscles. He repeated the same with the left side. Two deep bends backward and forward, finished with a set of toe touches, helped some. Each time he neared his cock, one image flashed through his mind—Joan between his legs, licking his balls and fondling his hardness. His fingers stroked the pre-cum leaking from his cock.

Coating the head, he rubbed his palm around his sensitive tip. His other hand cupped his balls, fondling them gently, adding pressure and friction to his actions. Turning slightly, he watched himself in the mirror. His voyeur side kicked in. He didn't care who he was viewing. Only that he could see the act in front of him mattered.

His grip tightened with each glide toward his balls, slicking his shaft with his growing wetness. He relaxed his hand on his upward stroke, stopping short of his cockhead. God, he loved the building need and slight buzz he got teasing himself along the edge of orgasming. The longer he waited, the more it built in intensity and rush. He was so close.

His eyes squinted, though he knew his reflection stared back, matching him stroke for stroke. There was a certain turn on seeing his pleasure acted out before him. If he closed his eyes, he'd lose his peak and the rough buildup to a hot, hard release. A few more strokes, and he'd be over the edge.

He bit his lip to prevent more sound from escaping. God, he was so damn close. "Yesss." He was going to...

A hard knock sounded on the door. David cracked open the door, asking, "Mason, mind if I come in?"

Shit, what did David want? Mason jerked his hands away from his cock and grabbed the towel closest to him. Wiping his palms, he tossed the towel on the floor like a bathmat and turned on the shower. His shampoo and soap sat on the edge of the shower's small rear shelf. The semi-opaque curtain offered cover and privacy. He'd rather David not catch him with a hard-on or start asking questions. "Give me a moment. I was just getting in."

Lukewarm water spattered his hand as he thrust it into the running water. Rather than waste time adjusting the temperature more, Mason jumped under the spray as he pulled the curtain shut.

"Come on in. What's up?" He hoped his voice sounded somewhat normal and maybe a bit tired.

David shut the door loudly. The click echoed briefly over the noise of the shower. He glanced around the bathroom. The cabinet-enclosed sink held four plastic-wrapped glasses and Mason's watch. David smiled at Mason's hastily strewn clothes.

"Joan and I are hungry. Since she's cooking, how about we come up with easy choices?"

"Uh, okay. What did you have in mind?" Mason's shadowed movements indicated he was hurrying through his shower.

"Slow down in there. You've got a few. How about a picnic theme? Sandwiches, fruit, and snacks with some wine. Toss some blankets and a few pillows on the floor."

"Sounds good to me. I'll be done shortly. Who's next?"

"Me. I'll hang up your uniform while you dry off. Leave the shower running, but cut back the heat. The steam is building up in here."

"Thanks. Leave my shorts, please."

David laid the hot red sleeping shorts atop the commode. Mason's flabbergasted look when he realized they were the only pair left in his size was a hoot. David smiled, thinking about what Joan's reaction would be when she saw them. Red was not one of Mason's favorite colors. Ah well, he'd have to make do for the next couple of days.

"Leave my boxers, too, please." Mason's drawn-out "please" sparked questions David decided to leave unasked. Poor man must be tired and dragged out. He didn't bother with underwear at home. David shut the door, leaving Mason to finish his shower in peace.

David faced Joan. Her gaze and shrug worried him. This wasn't her. What had her upset?

"Talk to me while I hang Mason's things up. He's almost done with his shower." David entered the closet and placed Mason's uniform pants and shirt on one hanger. His sweater went on another. "How about a picnic theme for dinner?"

"How much preparation are you expecting? I want a shower before I'm too tired to care or eat."

"What about finger foods and sandwiches? I can warm up the sandwiches while you shower. I already put the wine to chill, though scooping up some snow with the ice bucket might help."

Joan smiled and shook her head. "Ever practical. How is Mason helping?"

"Oh, leave that to me." David grinned and entered the bathroom, his blue shorts sticking out of his pants pocket.

Mason wrapped the towel tighter around his waist. He hated wearing boxers and shorts together. But the thought of asking David or Joan to hand him a pair of briefs set his stomach off, and his heart skipped a beat. At home with his roommate was one thing, but with Joan present was another. Why did he feel like he needed to be on his best behavior? A huge knot throbbed at the base of his neck. Sexual tension and need threatened to overcome his small reserve of self-control. Maybe he needed to eat and sleep.

David's hard knock hurried Mason's dressing. Tossing his damp towels on the floor, he smirked at his reflection. Hot red shorts with a hint of blue boxers peeking out below them. What a sight he made. It was too late to worry about it now.

"Who's next?" Mason called out, opening the door. David's nod and arched eyebrows tightened the knot growing across his shoulders and the new one forming in his groin. He wished David would come out and say what plans he had in mind. Asking him about his thoughts and views on Joan in the middle of Walmart had Mason wondering if David suspected his attraction to her. Was he trying to get him to admit it? What if he did? The one time he'd done so with another friend had gotten him a black eye, a busted lip and a ruined friendship. He didn't want that to happen nor lose Joan's friendship, either.

Catching Joan's tired gaze, Mason stepped aside and let David enter.

"Hang on one moment," David whispered as he passed.

Mason hung near the door, waiting to see what he wanted.

Chapter Three

David pushed the door partway closed and leaned toward Mason. "Help Joan out with making the sandwiches and offer to rub her feet once you're done. She's limping from wearing those heels all day. Surprise her with the slipper socks we got and see if she'd like a glass of wine before her shower."

Mason's silent nod and puzzled expression struck him as odd. Usually, they needed few words to communicate when their ideas ran in tandem. Was Mason tuning him out? Or being obtuse for a reason? David hoped Mason spoke up soon.

David clicked the door shut and shucked his hot, sticky clothes. Glad to be out of them, he entered the shower. Warm water cascaded over his head and down his front. Reaching for the shampoo, a scene unfolded in his mind. He wished Mason could pick up on his thoughts better. He'd be helping Joan relax very well if Mason caught on to this one.

Working the suds into his scalp, David closed his eyes and let his mind wander. His thoughts formed pictures, bringing one of his fantasies to life.

Joan stood before them, wearing a light, mauve-colored teddy. The white ribbon holding the top part closed laced down the front, ending just below her pert breasts. Thin straps covered her lightly tanned shoulders, and another bow sat at the rim of her pubis. As she turned, modeling the lingerie for them, the edge of the high-cut sides showed off her long legs and defined calves. He loved breasts, and Mason went for legs.

A slight turn more and her rounded firm buttocks came into view. The thong barely covered the cleft of her twin cheeks.

David grew harder as the fantasy played out in his mind. His soap-slicked hands stroked down his chest, stopping at his nipples. Plucking and twisting them, he groaned and rocked his hips back and forth. The scene in his head changed.

Joan walked toward him with a short leather quirt in her hand. She lashed the air, testing its stiffness and the cut of its movement. In her other hand, she held two clothespins. His nipples peaked, growing tauter the closer she came. Working his hand down over his stomach, he raked his nails around and across the sensitive area between his ribs and navel. He inhaled and bit his lip to keep his noise down. Pain edged his excitement higher. His cock jerked as Joan clamped first one nipple with a clothes pin, then his other nipple with the other clothes pin.

He grabbed his cock and squeezed. Exquisite torment raced up his shaft and pooled over his balls. Two more strokes and he'd orgasm. A hot, hard release...yes—Joan cracked the quirt against his ass and commanded he be quiet and service himself without further noise.

Soaping his hand, he quickly washed and treated himself to a small, fast orgasm. He soaped and rinsed again, cleaning away all traces of his sexual play. Having taken the edge off his horniness, David dried off and donned his shorts. He'd lucked out with a pair of lined lightweight sleep shorts. He didn't have to worry about briefs.

Opening the door, Joan's moans greeted him.

David reached down and adjusted the crotch of his shorts. Damn, he thought he'd taken the edge off his desire. One moan from Joan and his cock throbbed tight against his shorts.

"Oh, yes! That is so go–ooo–od!"

Joan's vocal punched him in the gut. What the hell was Mason doing? They hadn't discussed tactics beyond a foot massage and helping with dinner. He started through the doorway.

Two words echoed in his conscience—foot massage. He halted, his mouth open ready to speak. Should he peer around the wall and confirm what was happening? Announce his entrance?

What if they were doing something else? How should he handle it? He didn't mind, or did he? Being informed would be nice.

David sucked in his breath at Joan's next moan. He trusted Mason. Maybe there were limits to his trust. Their previous threesomes didn't involve someone this close to them, nor someone who cared as much about each other as they did.

David swallowed hard and shook his head. The sooner he knew what was happening, the better he'd feel. Sharing and knowing were one thing. Sharing and not having enough info was making him uneasy.

Clearing his throat, David stuck his head around the wall and grinned.

Mason looked up from where he knelt on the floor. Next to him sat Joan's bottle of cocoa butter and shea lotion. One slicked hand held her heel, and the other grasped her calf. She lay back propped on her elbows. Her broad grin and relaxed gaze slapped David's retort down his throat.

Joan sat up and touched Mason's shoulder. "Thanks, I needed that."

She rose and approached David. "He gives great foot rubs. Thanks for suggesting it."

She kissed his cheek and whispered, "Any hot water left?"

"Uhmm—yeah." He took in her glassy-eyed gaze, wondering what else had occurred while he showered.

"Thank you for the lovely slippers socks and robe," Joan murmured, patting his cheek.

She winked and sauntered into the bathroom, clutching the bag containing her gifts.

Robe? What robe? Mason hadn't said much in Walmart. Was he acting on his own? David clenched his hands and silently counted to ten.

Stop. Ask questions. Remember, he's your best friend. His conscience tried to thwart his ego and the green-eyed monster struggling to burst forth. Jealousy hadn't gripped him before. Why now? *Because you're in love with Joan. She's important in more ways than the other women ever were.*

Two words rolled through his thoughts—assume and quiet. He'd learned this fact not once but a few times before it sunk in. David wasn't blowing another friendship or relationship due to either assuming or keeping quiet.

The solid click of the door closing drew him from his musing. He shook his head and sat down at the table.

Mason rose and joined him. "I can see something is bugging you. Want to get it off your chest?"

"I'm not angry. Confused is probably a good word. What's with the robe?" He faced Mason and looked him in the eye.

"I didn't get a chance to tell you. I saw it hanging on a rack when I went to the pharmacy. It sorta matched the slippers. Sorry." Mason laid his hand out, palm up on the table. "I figured Joan might want an extra layer depending on what she brought to sleep in."

David inhaled deeply and smiled. "I sometimes forget how thoughtful you are. Thanks." He grasped Mason's hand and squeezed. "No hard feelings."

Joan pressed her ear to the door. Their muffled voices reached her. She couldn't make out what they said. Probably planning again. Eventually, they'd tell her. Even though she trusted them, she preferred knowing to not knowing. Too many past surprises had gone awry for her to be comfortable with them.

She smiled as she undressed, remembering a friend who had gifted her with a kitten shortly after she'd gotten her first place. Three days later, with a red nose, watery eyes, and a prescription for allergy pills, she'd returned the precious gray fur ball at arm's length to her friend.

Wiping steam off the mirror, she laughed. If she had appeared anywhere close to her current look, no wonder her friend had gasped. Red, tired eyes and mascara streaks greeted her, along with tufts of hair sticking out here and there. Okay, so at one point, she had laid back on the bed, clutching the spread, ready to cream her panties. Mason gave a damn good foot massage and knew the pressure points on her calves. Since he'd stopped hanging out much, she'd forgotten how good his hands felt on her.

A knock rattled the bathroom door. David cracked the door open and stuck his head in. "How much longer you gonna be, woman?" His teasing tone made Joan laugh.

"A bit longer. Why?"

"We'll get the picnic area ready. And open the wine if madam approves."

"Yes, and hand me my shampoo off the counter, please. I'll use one of your soaps."

David paused as her hand brushed his as she reached for the bottle. "Are you sure everything is all right?"

"Yes. Now go and let me shower." Joan pushed the door closed and turned the lock. A few moments without interruption, and maybe her calm would return. What was it about seeing a man's eyes light up with hot desire?

Since she began dating David, she'd grown accustomed to his presence. The nights he spent with her filled a part of her heart she hadn't noticed before. Still, the emptiness that used to be occupied by the three of them being together and sharing affectionate hugs and soft kisses refused to go away. Some nights she wanted to fall asleep wedged between Mason and David like they had sometimes sat together watching movies or talking about anything and everything.

Tearing open the bag sitting on the sink, Joan withdrew the slippers. Mauve-colored chenille footies greeted her. Their softness caressed her fingers. Reaching around behind her, she unhooked her bra. She almost groaned aloud as she slipped the straps down her shoulders and freed one breast, then the other. She arched her shoulders and rolled them, easing the tension working its way up her back.

Drawing the bag to her, she pulled out the lavender robe. Mason's thoughtfulness warmed her. White lace decorated the edges and button-up front. Its three-quarter-length sleeves made her smile deepen. He'd overheard her remark to David about borrowing one of his T-shirts to cover her pajama top and shorts sleep set. David had remembered her aching cold feet.

Most women considered themselves blessed to find one attentive, thoughtful, caring companion. She had two. Her heart skipped a beat as she looked in the mirror. Was she ready for the two of them?

A warm flush began just below her breasts and wormed its way upward. Images of Mason massaging her legs and feet flashed through her mind. She glanced at the slippers sitting on the edge of the sink. Their supple softness reminded her of his hands, his gentle yet firm grasp as he applied pressure against her calves and worked his knuckles across the soles of her feet. She thrust her hand into one slipper. Running her fingertips over the enticing softness, her cheeks grew warm at the thoughts racing through her mind. Vivid memories of a recent sensation play session with David formed and mixed with the images.

David tightened the silk scarf covering her eyes. "Can you see anything?" he asked huskily against her ear.

Excitement, tinged with a small amount of panic, rippled through her as something brushed against her. Her hands clenched and her arms flexed to rise. A cold ripple of fear iced across her stomach as her arms refused to move. Tipping her head from side to side, blackness greeted her. It was like she was totally blind and helpless. Never mind that she trusted the man she'd let restrain her in this way.

David's soft laugh rasped against her other ear. "Relax and let yourself adjust. In a few moments, your other senses will heighten, and the real fun begins."

She squirmed as he pulled her back against him. His hard cock nudged her buttocks and left a wet streak down one cheek. His hands cupped her breasts, rolling and tweaking her nipples between his fingers. Exquisite pleasure rippled over her, enveloping her deep within its web.

Heat pooled between her breasts and threatened to overflow any control she had. All she could do was feel. Panic chilled its way to the edge of her molten desire.

A tug and twirl. Then another and another in almost a steady rhythm until her sensitive tips tingled and pulsed at his slightest caress. His hot breath wrapped itself around the cool whorl of her ear and glided down over her arched neck. Shivers and trembles gripped her to her core as he raked his teeth slowly over her earlobe. "If you want me to stop, all you have to say is the code word."

A short rap on the door broke her attention.

Chapter Four

David's muffled laugh followed. "Joan, I think you forgot something," he called through the door.

Standing behind the door, Joan opened it and stuck her hand out. "Put it in my hand. I'll be out in ten minutes."

David stuffed her pajamas in her hand and kissed her wrist. "We'll be waiting."

Warmth pooled deep behind her navel and flooded outward. Stepping away from the door, her motion drew her eyes to the mirror. Her nipples stood firm, peaking out from her breasts as though they begged for attention. Dropping her gaze, the slippers came into view. The culprits called to her, beckoning one last caress and rub. One temptation she refused to resist.

Shoving her pajamas and robe aside, she grabbed and broke the plastic strip holding the slippers together. With one on each hand, she rubbed her cheeks and chin, luxuriating in the chenille's softness. Her eyelids drooped, and her hands slid down her throat and neck, raising more goose bumps along her arms and shoulders. Her hands moved lower until each stopped mid-breast. Taut and sensitized, her nipples pebbled, waiting their turn for caresses. Slowly, she inched her slipper-covered fingers forward, teasing along her areola and denying herself the full effect. Dare she go for it?

"Yes-ss," slipped from her pulled taut lips. Her hiss echoed softly and died as Mason's muted voice sounded outside the door. She dropped her hands and tossed the slippers atop her robe and pajamas. Thank goodness for the overhead heat lamp and exhaust fan. A short cold shower might help put out the wildfire building inside her.

David winked at Mason as he turned back from the bathroom door. "Something is going on in there."

Mason swallowed hard. He'd noticed the dampness of Joan's panties when she leaned back and clutched the spread as he massaged her feet. His ego and libido fought for dominance at that moment. What male could resist hearing a woman moan with pleasure and compliment him in the same breath? Hell, if his cock could have gotten any bigger, he'd have had two swollen heads to deal with. At least his cock knew how to let off some pressure. Good thing he'd worn his boxers and not forgone them. Or right now, he'd be explaining wet spots.

Damn, he'd forgotten how soft Joan's skin was and how sensual she was. Each touch and caress seemed to ignite a fuse between them. Touching her felt so right. It went beyond friendship. How much did he care? Could he explain or quantify it? He wasn't admitting too much until he found the words to describe his feelings. David and Joan's friendship meant more to him than a quickie or speaking out of turn.

Two swift knocks on the room's external door drew his and David's attention.

"Who is it?" David called out, tossing Mason a T-shirt.

"Manager," a male voice answered.

David walked toward the door, donning a T-shirt. He paused near Mason. "You might want to put that on to avoid the cold air when I open the door."

"Just a moment," he stated, watching Mason scramble into the shirt. He sidestepped as he opened the door. A gust of wind whipped in, sprinkling snow across his bare feet.

"Sorry to disturb you," the gray-haired gentleman explained. "We don't expect a power outage. But to be safe, I brought extra blankets and a couple of flashlights."

"Thanks. We appreciate it," Mason replied, reaching for the items.

"One more thing." The manager stepped back out and retrieved a large plastic shopping bag. "Clean towels and sheets for you. Storm's stalled. Hate to ask you to do your own housekeeping."

David laughed and took the bag. "Gives me a chance to practice my hospital corners."

As the manager turned, he pointed to the TV. "With the wind, reception is limited. Channel Eight is running an old movie marathon. Have a good night."

Locking the door, Mason turned. "Where are we picnicking?"

David glanced around the room. Only one area could accommodate them comfortably, the section closest to the bed. Talk about an obvious innuendo.

"Grab a couple of pillows off the bed and spread a blanket nearby. I'll check on Joan."

Mason stepped back from the picnic area. Two blankets, one on top of the other, formed a lopsided square. Pillows and glasses sat along the end closest to the door. The heater kicked on. Its whine and groan almost matched the wind's external noise.

"Nice." David's voice caught him off guard. Mason jumped, startled.

"Sorry about that," David began. "You sure you're all right?"

Mason shrugged. Blurting out an answer would destroy anything he already said to reassure them. If he didn't answer, David would start asking more questions he wasn't sure he could answer or wanted to. Yet they were stuck together for what now appeared to be two days, thanks to the damn storm. He'd better say something and sound convincing.

"It's been a while since the three of us got together. Just seems different, I guess."

David's muffled chuckle made him turn.

David sat on the edge of the bed. Mason's rigid shoulders and preoccupied look screamed of his edginess. Letting him speak might get his issue out in the open. "Look, something's bugging you. Spill it."

Mason's sigh punctuated his sideways glance. The last time he'd appeared this agitated was after his argument with his high school best friend.

David sucked in air. His stomach flip-flopped, sending an anxious ripple racing through his gut. His hands grew sweaty. Had he assumed when he needed to be direct? He rose as Mason sat facing him at the table. Clearing his throat, David made sure he had Mason's attention. "Tell me straight. What's going on?"

Mason's tight lips and shrug didn't help. Another belly flop and heart palpitation made him want to pace. "Want me to take a stab at it?"

Mason shook his head. "No thanks. I'm not sure I can put it into words."

"Okay, give it a try before Joan comes out." Anything was better than knowing nothing. Right?

Mason's nod slowed the agitation churning in his stomach and working its way into acidity, lapping up his throat. Their friendship ranked in importance as much as his and Joan's relationship. One more fast glance from Mason and he'd yell.

"All right, here it is," Mason started, rising and moving closer. The lock on the bathroom door clicked.

Shit, please don't let him clam up! David stood still, waiting to see if Mason continued.

"You and Joan are a couple. We've hung out very little since you began dating. Most times, I meet you at Joan's or you stay behind. It's awkward."

David rubbed his hands across his shirt, hoping to dry their sweatiness. He reached out and clasped Mason's shoulder.

"Joan's your friend. So am I. Just because we date hasn't changed that. Okay?"

"I guess. But..." Mason's voice trailed off as the bathroom door opened.

"Hey guys, where's the food?" Joan called out.

David stepped past Mason, gripping his shoulder. "Let's eat and kick back. We can talk more after we've eaten."

Mason nodded and moved toward the kitchenette. David caught his brief smile as Joan greeted him. Maybe he needed to hear it from both of them. They'd all been through changes in the last few months.

Mason's promotion moved him to longer flights. Joan's temporary duty status flexed her hours, sometimes daily. His own schedule was a whacked splits off or split shifts. None of them had much free time coordinating with the others. He could understand Mason's view. The last time he'd been this sullen, Mason had been in love.

Mason was in love—full out in love with—Joan? Or another woman and he felt guilty about it? Why? Loving Joan and another woman didn't subtract from love for each other. Except if Joan was his focus, what had him so wrought up?

David spun toward Mason. He stumbled. His lips moved though nothing came out. Joan caught his arm, righting him.

"A bit of wine already?" She winked at him and moved toward Mason.

"Let me help. That way we eat quicker," she offered, reaching for the bread.

Twenty minutes later, the TV announcer read the list of movies making up the marathon. Plates holding sandwiches, chips and pretzels, cut-up pieces of fruit and glasses filled with wine filled the space between them as the first movie began.

Mason stood and stretched. Three hours had gone by. Ninety-minute black-and-white movies had captured their attention as the mysteries unfolded. The remnants of their picnic dinner sat along the edges of the blanketed space. He smiled as Joan's hand flew to her mouth trying to cover another yawn. Turning, he clicked the TV off. David's soft chuckle drew Mason's attention. "What's so funny?"

"Joan's challenge that she'll outlast us on staying awake. Two movies down and she's yawning already." David nudged her.

"Hey, it's not my fault. A glass of wine and a full stomach...what do you expect?"

David rose and hovered over her. "How about we cut cards to see who cleans up?"

Mason sat on the edge of the bed. "Be great if we had a deck. Why not put our names on slips of paper, mix 'em up, and draw for who does what?"

Joan nudged David's leg as he groaned. "What's a matter, big boy?"

"I usually get stuck with the dishes."

Mason laughed. "Well, let's agree on three things, and the last one chosen gets to decide who they help."

"Besides," Joan added, "how long will it take to wash a few plates and forks?"

"Okay, okay." David threw up his hands. "I say the three things are dishes, trash, and what we do next."

"Agreed," Joan and Mason replied in unison.

David pondered Mason and Joan's interaction. He'd known Mason long enough to know the signs. And this time, he had it bad. The last time was with his ex-fiancée Betsy. Who'd captured his attention this time? How deep was his heart in it? He hoped Mason wasn't feeling guilty about caring for two women, Joan and his other interest.

Twenty minutes later, Joan handed David the last plate. "Can't you dry any faster?"

"Keep it up, woman, and you'll get yours." David stacked the plate atop the others sitting on the counter.

"Oh?" Joan grinned and turned. She took two steps and glanced over her shoulder.

"You crusin' for a towel swat?" David drew the hand towel tight between his hands.

"Have to catch me first." Joan picked up her pace and moved toward Mason. "You gonna let him get away with it?"

Mason's lopsided grin told her she was in trouble. A quick glance toward David showed he had closed the space between them.

Mason in front of her. David behind her. Crap! If she didn't do something quick...

Out of the corner of her eye, she spied her backup. Mason had left the pillows on the foot of the bed as they cleaned up. Grabbing the closest one, she spun toward David.

"Pillow fight!" Joan yelled and smacked the towel between his hands.

"Help, Mason," David yelped as Joan came back around.

"She's lethal with that thing. I ain't getting near it."

Two quick *thwacks* sounded as Joan and David swatted at each other. Mason leaned on the doorjamb and glanced at his watch.

"Let me know when you're done." He feigned a yawn and looked up.

Mistake! Joan and David advanced toward him.

Holding up his hands in front of him, he stepped sideways. "Wait a minute."

Joan moved away from him. He turned his head, keeping her in sight.

Smack! David's laughter followed close behind him. Joan snickered and stuck out her tongue at him.

"I yield," Mason yelped.

A loud thud sounded. "Damn," David cussed.

Mason turned toward him. David lay sprawled across the floor with the remaining pillows scattered around him.

Joan burst out laughing as she plopped down next to David. "Never underestimate a woman and her arsenal."

David made a face at her and joined in her laughter. Mason soon joined in.

Chapter Five

Joan knuckled a tear from her cheek. "God, I needed that. I haven't laughed that hard in a while."

David wiped his eyes with the hem of his shirt. "Yeah, sometimes it feels good to be silly."

Mason sat down opposite them, holding out a box of tissues. His other hand held two, damp from wiping his eyes. "Need these?"

Joan pulled several from the box and handed David some. "Thanks. Whew. I'm thirsty."

David dragged his improvised ice bucket closer—a small wastebasket a third full of melted snow. He drew the almost empty wine bottle from it. "How about this?"

"Hey, you're getting me wet." Joan scooted closer to Mason. "How are we supposed to drink it? Out of the bottle?"

David shoved the bottle back into the wastebasket. It wobbled back and forth. He started to stand, taking hold of the basket, causing it to rock more.

"I don't think that is a good idea," Joan warned, sliding further away.

"Hang on." Mason stood. "I'll get a towel and some glasses."

He picked up the basket and headed to the kitchenette. After dumping the water out, he sat the wastebasket beneath the counter. He returned with the towel-wrapped bottle and three clean glasses.

"What's next?" he asked, filling their glasses. "Another movie?"

"Maybe, if one of the other channels works." Joan started to reach for the remote.

"Maybe a game," David offered, twisting the empty bottle between his hands.

Joan fingered the remote, glancing back and forth at Mason and David. What was running through David's mischievous mind? His grin and wink at her indicated his thoughts ran in a direction she wasn't sure she understood. Mason appeared to be at ease with David's suggestion. He leaned on his hands with his legs stretched out in front of him, smiling. Had they finally talked and had a meeting of the minds? Joan took a sip of wine and swallowed.

"Uhmmm—what did you have in mind?" she ventured, hoping she wasn't getting in over her head.

"Oh, nothing too hard." David laid the bottle on its side between them and spun it. "Remember Spin-the-Bottle?"

Mason groaned. "God do I. Try kissing a girl with a mouth full of braces and not get yours locked up with hers."

"Yeah, you and Missy Snider." David chuckled and stopped the spinning bottle. "No, not quite that bad. How about a version of it, but we up the ante?"

Joan bit her lip to keep from snickering at the look on Mason's face. His mouth opened and shut while his eyes widened. Whatever David had cooked up, he hadn't told Mason. Maybe they could still back out.

"Explain, please. I'm holding back my answer till I know more." She crossed her arms tight against her chest. She probably shouldn't have any more wine.

David explained his game idea. But what was this about the bottle and kissing or answering a question? "Go over that again."

"Yeah," Mason added. "I wanna make sure I got this right."

David sighed. "Okay, we're doing Spin the Bottle with a twist. If it lands on Mason when I spin it, instead of kissing him, I can answer a question. You or he can ask it. If it lands on one of us and you don't want to kiss us, you can answer a question. Got it?"

Joan looked from Mason to David. Mason's shrug and nod didn't help. At least she hadn't gotten in over her head so far. "Yes. It doesn't seem hard."

David's grin grew. He almost smiled. Joan pulled her knees to her chest. Maybe she'd better take back that last thought.

"Wait. There's more."

Joan groaned and hugged her knees tighter to her. Mason shifted his position and glared at David.

"The question must be in the form of truth or dare." David looped his fingers together behind his head and kept on grinning.

"Well, I'm game," Mason stated. "But instead of dare, how about strip?"

"*Strip?*" Joan spit out.

"Yes, since dares you usually can do within reason. How can we in this small space? We've got lots of clothes."

Joan squirmed and looked from Mason to David. Both of them watched her intently.

"All right, here's my condition then. Each round is five turns and only two kisses can be chaste, like a peck on the cheek or lips. I get to choose how long the kiss lasts and number of them. Maybe even a French kiss or two as the game goes on."

She wasn't sure how long they stared at each other as if one of them waited for the other to give in. By now, the rest of the wine had to be sneaking up on the guys as well. Maybe they'd all chicken out. Or would they?

"So if the bottle lands on Joan, either she answers a question truthfully, kisses one of us, or strips an article of clothing. If it lands on one of us, we answer the question or strip unless Joan is the one spinning the bottle."

Mason paused and drew in a deep breath. He tried to swallow. His dry throat refused to cooperate. It wanted to constrict every time his stomach fluttered.

"That's right. I'm ready. How about you?" David glanced at Joan and then him.

Mason caught Joan's quick nod as she stood. He grabbed his glass out of her way.

"Good." David rubbed his hands together. "And you?"

Mason gulped hard. Joan took off her robe, revealing her top and shorts pajamas. The shorts clung to her buttocks from her sitting down. His gaze continued down her legs, noting each curve and dip. What was it about a gorgeous pair of feminine legs that got him going?

Joan teased David. "No, I'm not stripping already. I'm gonna put more layers on before I start playing this game."

Joan tossed her robe on the bed. "Mason, you've been awfully quiet. What do you think about putting on more clothes before we start playing?"

"Uhm-m-mm. Sure. Why not?" He tried swallowing again. If he put on enough clothes, maybe he could avoid answering questions or kissing Joan more than a couple of times each round. Hell, he'd love to French kiss her and get her lush curves against him.

Mason glanced at David. Had he caught on to his feelings about Joan? David's willingness to share other women at the same time didn't bother him. But they weren't involved with them. A few they knew as mutual friends. Others they'd known separately, and things had happened on an impromptu basis. How would David react with Joan? Past experience knotted Mason's gut.

"All right," David stated, "more clothes it is, but..."

Joan stopped two steps from him. Mason didn't like the smirk curling his lips.

"...no more than three shirts, two shorts or sweat pants plus underwear, and two pairs of socks." David moved to the edge of the bed. "Joan, your robe can count as one layer if you like."

Mason rose and faced them. "Okay, then we can remove one sock at a time and have it count. Jewelry doesn't count."

"You're on." Joan burst out laughing and rushed toward the closet. "I call dibs on a T-shirt from each of you and a pair of David's socks."

Twenty minutes passed as each added layers and discarded unwanted items. Joan sat beside David wearing one of his oversized T-shirts beneath her robe; Mason's smaller one made up her top layer. Velour pants and David's socks along with her slippers socks completed her outfit.

David added two pairs of socks and a couple more shirts. Sweat pants and a pair of briefs finished off his layers.

Mason sat on the floor, struggling to pull on his second pair of socks. "Now I remember why I hated wearing two pairs of socks as a kid."

His unbuttoned uniform shirt moved as he worked to settle comfortably between David and Joan. Under it, he wore two shirts and sweatpants over his shorts and boxers.

Joan giggled each time he squirmed. "Ants in your pants?" she teased.

"Nah. Settling everything in the right place." He blew a raspberry at her as she tugged her robe back on her shoulder.

"Foul. I saw your pajama top under there. You got an extra layer," he countered.

"Yeah, cuz your bare chest is acceptable. Mine isn't, so I get to keep it."

David cleared his throat and sat the bottle between them. "If Joan gets to the point of losing her last layer, shorts and top, she has to shuck both, okay? Or she loses a kiss, type of our choice."

"I guess so," Joan replied, shrugging.

"Mason?" David spun the bottle. "Your answer before it stops. After that, the game begins. No more changes."

The bottle began to slow. Mason could feel both of them watching him, waiting for his answer. One last turn and...

"Fine," he blurted out. The bottle pointed to him. Shit, now he had to go first?

His gaze rose to David. "I ain't kissing you."

David laughed and handed him the bottle. "No, you get to spin first. And I ain't kissing you either. Not even buzzed."

"I think we're all buzzed," Joan offered, leaning back against the bed and yawning.

"Think you can stay awake?" David challenged.

"Oh, yeah, cuz I'm not losing." She sat upright. "Spin the bottle, Mason."

He laid the bottle on its side and spun it hard. Around it went. Once, twice, thrice and began slowly turning back toward him.

David waited until the bottle stopped near Mason. "One last change. If it lands back on you, you can pass, spin again, or put back on a piece of stripped clothing."

"I pass." Mason picked up the bottle and handed it to Joan. "Your turn."

Three spins later, Mason breathed easier. Joan was down a slipper, David one sock, and he'd gotten a chaste peck on the cheek from Joan. His turn again. The bottle pointed at David.

"Gonna lose something or try a question?" David queried. The glint in his eye sent a slight chill across Mason's shoulders.

"Sock off." Mason peeled one off and grinned. "Your turn."

David spun and chuckled as the bottle stopped near Mason. "Other sock?"

Mason handed over the mate.

"Two more spins, and the round is over," Joan crowed.

"Yes, and two chances you could lose a couple more pieces of clothing or up the kiss type," David countered.

Mason knew David loved competing and challenges. He probably calculated the odds of losing versus winning in his steel-trap mind. Few saw or knew that side of him. David preferred to take a softer and laid-back approach to life. Did Joan realize she'd challenged him?

Mason glanced at David as he handed Joan the bottle. He winked and barely nodded before turning back to Joan. "I believe it's your turn."

Joan sighed and spun the bottle. Damn David and his competitive streak. She had one chaste kiss left along with two full on the lips or a French one still at her disposal. She turned her attention to the slowing bottle.

Maybe she'd French Mason. The thought made her stomach flutter, and a warm glow flowed over her lower half. She'd forgotten how his washboard abs and toned pecs turned her on. David was firm and muscular. Mason's defined male curves heated her libido in a different way.

The bottle swung past Mason. Or would she end up kissing David? He just might end up with his sock instead.

"Oh ho." David laughed. "It seems the bottle has yet to decide." It slowly passed him and inched toward her.

Joan held her breath, knowing her decision. "I—"

The bottle rolled by her.

"Mason's the man." David's tone irked her. She swore he intended to toss her to Mason. How dare he without asking!

Right, her conscience chided. *You've wanted Mason. Here's your chance, or are you chicken?*

Chapter Six

Joan hesitated in announcing her decision. If she did French kiss Mason, would David lay off and let things happen on their own? Perhaps she needed to ask a question and start them talking about things. Still, without knowing how David might react, she wondered if tossing caution to the wind was a good option.

Rather than risk it all, she decided to chance a full-on-the-lips kiss and see how either reacted.

"Mason, slide over here and pucker up." She patted the area next to her.

She snuck a glance at David, hoping to catch his uncensored response. He grinned and leaned back on his hands, while folding his legs in front of him. Turning to Mason, she smiled and crooked a finger at him.

"I don't bite. If I do, I promise it won't show...much." She drew out the last word and snickered. "Well?"

Mason scooted over and leaned toward her, lips puckered and his eyes wide open. He arched his eyebrows up and down as he tilted his head more.

Joan met him partway and pressed her lips tight to his. Her hand lightly gripped his shoulder to steady him. His eyes took on a glow and intent look about them as though he wanted to tell her something but wouldn't voice it aloud. Or was he trying to read her mind? Either way the glow vanished as she blinked.

Pulling back, she inhaled and withdrew her hand. Sparks and tingles kept rushing up and down her arm. Her nipples tightened, and she grew warm. If a kiss on the lips did this, what would French kissing do? She sure as hell wanted to find out. David's cough shattered her further thoughts.

"Mason, you're next."

Mason spun the bottle and moved back to his original space. It pointed to David.

"I'll take a question," David ventured. Several moments passed without anyone speaking. "How about either of you coming up with one?"

"I've got one," Joan offered.

"Go ahead."

"How do you feel about Mason's and my kiss?"

David caught his bottom lip between his teeth. He worried it back and forth a few times and sat forward. Mason reminded himself to breathe and remember David was not like his prior friends. Yet a certain amount of trepidation bubbled through his stomach.

"Honest reaction, right?" David looked at Joan and glanced at Mason.

"Yes," Joan answered.

"No biggie. I've seen you two hug and kiss before."

"But on the lips?" Mason grabbed his glass and downed the last of his wine. Voicing his curiosity aloud like that. Shit, he hoped he hadn't blown it.

"So what? Joan chose to kiss you, and you responded. It's not like I own her. We're all friends." Mason watched David's face as he spoke. Some of his uneasiness came through the way his eyes darted back and forth from Joan to him. Maybe more needed to be said? Discussed?

"Okay, my turn now." David reached for the bottle and spun it. "Last spin this round. Shall we up the ante next round and two pieces of clothing or two questions if you don't kiss?"

Mason's hand shook as he sat his glass down. What was David doing? Did he really think the two of them were going to start smooching? Or fondling each other?

"What do you mean up the ante?" Joan blurted out. She wrapped her arms tighter around herself.

"Relax, okay?" David chuckled and stretched his legs out in front of him. He kicked the bottle, sending it rolling toward Mason.

"Hey, that voids the turn," Mason countered, picking up the bottle.

"Fine by me," David responded. His smile grew as he caught Joan squirming out of the corner of his eye. "Joan?"

"Yeah." Her glum look and dull tone cut him to the quick.

"Why the look?" he asked, kissing her cheek.

"Are you making changes so you can win or...?" Joan stopped speaking.

"Or what?" David prompted. Had she figured out his plan? Joan could be a sore loser. She didn't mind not winning. It was his competitive streak. She compared it to stacking the deck or cheating. The outcome of the game was determined before play began. Where was the fun or the challenge then?

Joan sighed and nodded at Mason. "Sorry, Mason. David, are you tossing me at him?"

David watched their faces for a few moments before he spoke. Mason's bug-eyed look and the frantic shaking of his head drew Joan's attention. "No, I'm not tossing you at each other. We're all good friends. I don't see anything wrong with some sensual play."

"Sensual?" Mason rasped.

"A few kisses and hugs amongst friends. What's wrong with that?" David shrugged and moved his legs to the edge of the blankets.

"How far do you plan on this going?" Joan shot him a scowl.

"As far as we're all comfortable. No more. I'm tired of us being at odds with each other."

David turned to Mason. "How do you feel?"

"I–I'm—" Mason looked away as he finished. "Unsure."

"See," Joan started, "that's what I'm talking about."

"Hold on." David held up his hand. "Are you saying you're uncomfortable around Mason?"

"No, but—"

"No buts," David interrupted her. "What about you, Mason? Do you feel uncomfortable around either of us?"

"As a couple, yes."

Joan's gaze snapped to Mason. "You what?"

"Since you began dating, things have changed." Mason shrugged. "One-on-one, I'm fine. We're friends."

"I don't get how things changed." Joan wanted to fold her arms and tuck her hands under her arms, but then David would know she was fussing and smoldering.

"Once you and David switched over to a couple, things became twoish. No longer three. I feel like a third wheel sometimes." Mason leaned back on his hands. Joan angled herself to see his face better.

"Go on," David picked up the bottle. Joan glanced at him to be sure she caught his body language, tone, and words.

"Being the odd man out hangs like an anchor around my neck. I want to be free to touch Joan and be like we've always been. Then I stop because I don't want to piss you off, David." Mason nodded as Joan shrugged again.

"I don't want to ruin our friendship or lose my best friend. But you're a hottie, Joan. What guy wouldn't want to kiss you?"

David set the bottle between them and spun it. "Let's change tactics. If the bottle lands on a guy, they have to answer a question or strip. If we choose to strip, two pieces of clothing get forfeited. If it lands on Joan, she kisses us both the same or she strips two pieces."

"Trying to level things?" Joan glanced at him and turned to Mason. "What do you think?"

David picked up the bottle, getting their attention. Before Mason could reply, David spoke. "Yes, I'm leveling things. We never agreed to exclusivity. If you were to see someone else, I'd prefer Mason because I trust him."

"Thanks." Mason leaned over and kissed Joan's cheek. He slid his arm around her waist and squeezed.

"You're welcome." David's soft smile reached his eyes. Mason's anxiety cooled a few degrees.

His head spun from the wine he'd hastily gulped. David's last statement blew him away. He hoped he didn't violate that trust. Now if he could hold his tongue until the effects of the wine wore off, he'd be in good shape.

Joan took the bottle from David. "So you're fine with me kissing Mason like I do you? My choice?"

Mason's stomach flopped twice with each erratic heartbeat. What the hell was Joan doing? Playing with fire? Plucking David's nerve? His gaze froze on David.

David nodded and grinned. He pointed at the bottle. "Sure. Spin."

Joan turned the bottle so it pointed at Mason. She cocked her wrist and spun the bottle hard in a counterclockwise direction.

Her quick wink and small grin did nothing to quiet Mason's queasy stomach or slow his rapid heart rate. Who was tossing whom at whom? Was Joan admitting her interest? Or David tossing him to her? Christ, how had this turned into a game of one-upmanship? And David's statement he was fine with Joan smooching him the same way she did David...

Mason swallowed hard and reminded himself to take deep breaths. Actions spoke louder than words. He hoped no one bore grudges come game's end or in the morning.

The bottle's blur started to slow. As it spun by him again, he looked from Joan to David, wondering what their thoughts were.

"Ah ha!" Joan's growing smile and amused look sent his innards racing into overdrive. His gaze dropped to where she pointed.

"David," she began, drawing out his name. "Question or strip?"

Mason swallowed twice, hoping to avert a hiccup. Instead, a low-toned burp pushed past his taut lips. "Excuse me."

Joan's scrunched forehead and determined stare almost made him laugh. He knew that look all too well. But damn, did he have to be fodder for their two-edged competitive streaks?

Oh well, if he had any choices, his was to kiss Joan and cop a feel or two. Might as well enjoy himself.

"Well, David?" Joan asked.

"Strip." David shrugged out of his uniform shirt and pulled off a sock. "My turn."

His spin landed on Mason. "I still ain't kissing you," he quipped, sticking out his tongue. "Your choice."

Mason handed over two more socks. His spin landed on Joan. He wet his lips, hoping she'd choose kiss. His curiosity refused to be placated any longer. Time had come for him to enjoy the game.

Joan stifled another yawn. He wasn't too far behind her. The effects of the wine began reaching the rest of him. A sense of relaxation ebbed and flowed the sleepier he felt. His eyes felt gritty, and he wanted to close them.

"So kiss or strip," David prompted and snickered. "I think Mason's already decided for you."

"Huh?" Mason jumped, and his eyes flew open. Damn, he'd shut them and practically dozed off.

"Hmm–m–m–m–m." Joan twittered. "I think I'll kiss both of you."

"Think you're up to it?" David winked and leaned forward.

David's leer sent a shiver down Mason's back. Joan's making a face in response didn't help either. He'd swear these two had a private challenge going on. How the hell had he ended up in the middle?

"Yes I am, and Mason gets the first kiss." Joan held out her hand and faced him.

Mason leaned toward her and offered his cheek.

"No. Face me, please."

Mason's throat and mouth went dry. He could feel every beat of his heart. Joan inched closer.

"Put your legs out in front of you. I'm gonna sit on your lap." She scooted tight to him and rose on her knees.

"You sure you're okay with this?" he asked, eyeing David.

David's silent nod sent ripples through his jittery stomach and a new hiccup rattling up his throat. He tried taking a deep breath, hoping to thwart the ensuing result. No such luck. "Hic! Hic!"

Joan giggled and cupped his cheek as she moved closer. "Poor Mason. It's all right. Joan's gonna kiss you and make it all better."

Make it all better? His cock leapt out of deep slumber and stood at attention, wanting to get in on the action. Swell, now he had a hardon to explain. Leave it to his quirky sense of humor to kick in. His ego chided, *"Yeah, Joan, wanna kiss that and make it better, too?"* Sometimes Mason wondered if he had a huge masochistic streak or a sadistic one; either way, he bore the brunt of both.

Chapter Seven

"How about a glass of water first?" Mason grinned and stretched his legs out in front of him. "Make yourself comfortable, madam, while David gets my water."

He flashed David a cheesy grin and winked before helping Joan onto his lap.

David rose, sauntering into the kitchenette. He chuckled, shaking his head. A quick glance back at Joan and Mason widened his growing smile.

Joan sat on the edge of Mason's lap with her arms around his neck. They were nose-to-nose. David could see part of Mason's face. A half smile softened his face. Good, at least maybe Mason had begun to lighten up and enjoy the sensual play.

Filling a glass with water, David returned to the blanketed area, offering it to Mason. "Here ya go. And is there anything else I can get while I'm up?"

"Thanks, David. I'd like some water, too. Why not fill up one of the empty half-liter soda bottles and grab a couple more glasses?" Joan took the glass from Mason and sat it on the floor next to her. "I'll wait till you're settled to kiss Mason."

Turning back to Mason, she asked, "Are you all right now?"

"Yes. Could you move over a bit more? My leg is cramping up in this position." Mason tried to shift Joan from the edge of one leg to fully on his lap. He hoped his cock decided to behave. All bets were on that not happening.

Joan moved across his legs, rubbing her tight buns over and against his horny cock. He hoped her two layers between them buffered some of the poking and prodding his bad boy was intent on trying.

She ducked her head to avoid hitting his chin. He caught David's amused look over the top of her head. His slight nod and thumb-up motion told Mason his earlier worst thoughts weren't necessary.

David sat next to them and grinned. Mason shrugged, drawing Joan's attention.

"Is something wrong?" She withdrew her arms from around his neck.

"No, you're fine. Did you want water now or after we kiss?" Mason nodded at David.

"Now, please." Joan smiled at David, returning his smile. Sitting on Mason's lap felt right. Yet, part of her kept shaking a finger at herself. It didn't worry her. She knew David's trust in Mason ran high and didn't come lightly. So why not relax and enjoy the kiss?

David handed her a half-full glass of water. She drank several swallows before handing it back. "Thank you."

Licking her lips, she tilted her head, turning to Mason. "Put your arms around me," she huskily whispered, putting hers back around his neck.

Mason obliged and pulled her closer, nestling her against his chest. At this angle, she was tight to him. Something nudged her buttocks as she squirmed.

"Uh-uh," Mason groaned. "Easy, please. Certain parts of my anatomy don't take chafing lightly."

"Sorry," she offered. "But I do like your reaction." She stroked his cheek, leaned closer, closing her eyes and puckering her lips.

Mason's lips grazed hers and then settled firmly upon them. His arms slid up her back midway between her shoulders and waist. Moving her hands up his neck, she fingered his hair. Its softness ran between her fingers and onto her hands as she slid them deep into his hair.

Mason fitted his mouth more tightly to hers. Joan peeked through her lashes, confirming his eyes were closed as well. Part of her wondered if he fantasized about another girl or if he was savoring the experience as much as she was.

Arching her fingers, she wove her hands deeper into his hair, scratching her nails lightly along his scalp. Mason's muffled "yes" parted his lips. Joan didn't hesitate and went for it. Matching her lips to his, she nestled the tip of her tongue between his lips. His reaction dictated her next move.

Mason pulled her to him, pressing them tighter together. His tongue met hers briefly. They dueled, testing how far the other would venture until a full French kiss was upon them. His hands roved up and down her back, massaging and caressing. Each time her tongue drew back, his followed boldly, courting hers, accepting no retreat. She could feel his cock swell and nudge her the more they kissed. Her nipples had to be as hard as he was.

David's muffled cough drew them apart. "I'd say save some for me, but I'm not sure there's any left."

Joan tucked her hair behind her ears as she rested her forehead against Mason's. She watched his eyes, looking for a sign of his reaction.

He blinked several times and stared as though he looked past her or his thoughts were elsewhere. She inhaled and spoke. "Are you okay?"

Mason nodded, rubbing his lips together. His nostrils flared each time he inhaled. He pulled back, creating some space between them. "Yeah, thanks."

She lifted her buttocks, attempting to move off Mason's lap.

"Easy, please," Mason whispered, grimacing with each move. "Maybe David can stop snickering long enough to lend us a hand."

Joan glanced over her shoulder. "Oh, I think he owes us that much. His turn is next."

David stood and helped Joan to her feet. Drawing her into his arms, he kissed her quickly. "You sure you're ready?"

She swallowed hard. His eyes glowed with his usual competitiveness. Yet, there was a difference. She pressed tighter against him, needing the reassurance of his touch and warmth. He settled deeper into the hug, his head dipping toward her. His legs parted, almost straddling hers, allowing their lower halves to fit against each other. She stepped closer, tightening her hold on him. He rocked against her.

"You've got a hardon," Joan gasped and tried to move back. David held her firm, preventing her separation.

"Who wouldn't after watching you two? Dang, the heat rolled off you and caught me in its ripple." David rubbed his hands across her shoulders.

He stopped at her waist. Snuggling her, he whispered, "Let's see if we can catch Mason in our ripple."

"But he's already got one." Joan dipped her head. She was sure her face must be red, considering the heat she felt running up her neck.

"Oops, sorry," Mason offered, his voice tinged with laughter.

"I'm sure he does." David's hand left her back and cupped her cheek. His hand slid down her jaw, stopping at her chin. She tried to free herself from his grasp.

"What makes you think he wants to lose it?" David teased, tipping her head back to meet his gaze.

"I–uh–I—" she stammered.

God, she sounded like an inexperienced youth. She felt like one in some ways. Kissing Mason turned her on more than she expected. She'd fantasized about wrapping her arms around him and laying an intense lip lock on him, but damn, the heat flowing through her once they'd begun Frenching had practically boiled her dry.

Wow, she'd like to—no, make that love to—kiss Mason like that again and again. That could be addicting. Yet, David's reaction wasn't what she'd expected.

Sure, he'd said he didn't mind. Part of her believed his words. Another part refused to accept it. Her experience said otherwise. David's chuckle broke her train of thought.

"Joan, did you enjoy kissing Mason, knowing I watched you?" David held her chin firm, gazing into her eyes. He winked and smiled. "Be honest. It's okay. I enjoyed it. Did you?"

Joan looked down, averting her eyes, and nodded.

"Maybe Mason would enjoy watching?"

"Sure, why not?" Mason chimed in.

Joan drew a deep breath and exhaled. Her conscience pinged less loudly the more she repeated David's words and Mason's earlier pronouncements about her being a hottie.

David released her chin. She caught Mason's smile when she glanced at him. It was surely different. How far would they go? Could she go?

"So you're both comfortable sharing?" There, she'd voiced her concern and curiosity.

"So far, yes," David responded. "No biggie. Why?"

"I don't want to lose us either." Joan turned in David's arms to face Mason. "Yours and my friendship means a lot to me. I like the three of us."

Mason smiled from where he sat and offered his hand. "I do, too. He pointed to his shorts. "But my tent pole is rapidly wilting here."

David rubbed his hips against her buttocks. "Hmmmm, I think I am, too. What ya gonna do about it, woman?"

"Oh, I'm responsible?" Joan questioned, turning sideways in David's arms, keeping Mason in view.

"Well, Mason isn't. That's for sure." David settled her against him.

"Oh, kiss him and see what you can do," Mason challenged. He moved toward the corner of the bed. "Maybe I should sit on the bed to make sure I get a good view?"

"Smart-mouth." David grasped her waist, turning her completely to him. "Get your view settled, buddy. The show's started."

Heat grew in intensity as David's hand slid to her hips. He rocked and rubbed against her, mimicking what he'd do if they were nude. Joan gasped as he fluttered his hand upward, tracing the cleft of her buttocks, working toward the small of her back.

Oh, Lord, he was going for her sweet spot where the indentation of the small of her back dipped toward her upper torso. She sucked in air as his fingers lightly tapped along the top of her hips just short of the area he sought. Warmth grew with each tap, sending short tingles shooting through her. His other hand stoked up her hip and massaged her waist.

Joan inhaled deeply as his nails lightly raked over her waist, moving closer to his other hand. Her eyelids grew heavy and threatened to close. Heat rose deep from within and rushed over her, enveloping her from head to toe. His hand held her tight to him, circling and caressing the outer edge of her sweet spot. Regardless of which way she moved, his hot groin stoked the heat building within her.

Joan blinked, hoping to cool the growing need rippling through her. Arching her neck, she caught Mason's interested gaze. Her view dropped lower. His hard-on had returned.

"I believe the pyrotechnics are about to begin." David's head dipped to hers.

He nibbled her bottom lip, drawing it into his mouth as he ground against her, building more heat between them.

David pulled back and turned them to face Mason. "Hot enough for you, my friend?"

His hand traced upward, outlining Joan's ass and hips. He bunched her robe in his hand, inching its hem up, revealing more and more of her toned calves and defined thighs.

"Like what you see?" David pulled her robe tight across her ass and dipped her back over his other arm.

"So plump and ready for swatting. What you think?"

All these questions to Mason. What is he doing?

Joan gasped as David leaned her farther back. She swallowed hard at the look in his eye. She swore his blue eyes changed color each time he touched her or spoke. It was as though his little show turned him on as much as he was hoping to do so to Mason.

"Damn, I only kissed her." Mason's voice sounded strained and garbled. She tried twisting her head to get a better view. Her knees wobbled, and she stumbled toward Mason. David caught her and...swat!

"Be still and behave," David warned.

Joan blinked and tossed her head. Warmth crept across her buttocks cheek, adding to her rapidly raising internal temperature. Where was David going with all this? She wet her lips, ready to voice her concerns. When had kink entered into the game?

"Yes, and I kissed her, too. But a little extra heat never hurts. Wanna join in?" David's chuckle should have sent cold shivers racing over her and cooled her off. Instead, coupled with Mason's response, her knees gave way, thrusting her against David.

"Yes," Mason hissed, rising to his feet. "I can see a Joan sandwich happening."

Chapter Eight

"Front or back?" David offered, steadying Joan.

"You have a preference?" Mason countered, moving close enough that she could feel his heat.

Joan licked her lips and tried to swallow. Her throat constricted as she inhaled.

God, had David been reading her mind or peeking into her fantasies? Not that he could. But still—one of her ultra-secret ones was possibly about to come true.

"I think maybe Joan should decide." David touched her arm. "Well, madam, what do you say?"

"Huh?" Joan blurted out, startled by David's touch.

Boy, did she sound stupid. *Two hunkish men are about to sandwich me between them, and all I can say is "huh"!*

"Easy, it's okay," David soothed, running his hand up and down her arm.

Mason's breathy chuckle caressed her cheek. "Yeah, it's just us. You ready?"

He stepped closer, his hand entwined with hers.

"Oh, yes," she whispered. "You choose."

Mason slid behind her and slipped his arms around her waist, pulling her back to him. He nestled between her legs so she straddled his feet. "Next."

Leaning into him, she rested her shoulders on his chest. Every breath he took brought some part of them in contact and enhanced the hot sparks coursing through her. David had primed her sweet spot all right and turned her thermostat on high.

Looking up at him, she caught his lust and shivered. His hands reached toward his shorts.

"Is it hot in here? Or is it me?" he quipped, stepping toward her.

Responses fled her mind. Mason's hands roamed between her ribs and hips, moving nearer her mons and breasts with each stroke.

David slowly inched his left hand up Joan's arm, lightly scratching the exposed areas of her inner wrist and elbow with his nails. He gathered her free hand in his other and intertwined their fingers.

His eyes never left hers as he closed the space between them. As his hand reached her shoulder, he glanced down. Her eyes followed his movement and blinked at the object impeding his progress.

"We don't need this anymore." He kicked the bottle aside and settled between her open legs, lightly pressing against her.

He could feel Mason's hands rubbing up and down her ribs and stomach. He'd stopped short of her pubis and breasts. Joan's jagged breaths and short sighs said she enjoyed what he did. Her short moans as he stroked away indicated she wanted more.

David knew how to push her pleasure higher and to more intense levels. Mason didn't. How did David guide him, short of words or putting his hands on his to show him what Joan enjoyed and wanted? If this was going to work, they all needed to be engaged.

"Tell us what you want," David whispered, his lips close to Joan's ear.

"What?" Tingles from David's warm breath coursed down her neck, sending her pulse racing and making her nipples tauter.

"Guide us. Help us pleasure you." David's hot words against her ear sent her imagination downward.

Two sets of warm, masculine hands caressed almost every part of her. Could she coherently tell them what she wanted? Needed?

"Touch me," she rasped. She tried opening her eyes to locate whose hands were whose. But, her own desire held her tight within its grasp. Her lids fluttered shut as their hands met near her breasts.

"We are." Mason's breath warmed her right ear.

"Yes." David's response heated her other.

"Follow each other together." Her voice trailed off to a whisper, leaving her last words beyond audible range.

"Oh, follow the leader. One of my favorite games." David's husky tone vibrated against her neck, sending hard, hot tendrils of need deep into her. His tongue laved over her earlobe, catching it between his teeth.

"My turn," Mason mumbled, copying David's actions.

Where one left off, and the other began, she couldn't tell. She gave herself over to the sensations coursing through her. It was as though the guys moved in unison.

Mason moved firmly against her, rubbing his hard cock lightly against her ass. He didn't quite penetrate the crack of her cheeks. Hot desire raced over her like lava escaping a volcano. Her belly tightened with need, and her nether lips swelled, separating as her own wetness trickled forth. He rocked back and forth against her, imitating what he'd do sans clothes.

Longing and want threatened to claim her and pull her deeper into her own growing desire. Joan rocked her hips forward, needing space to catch her breath. She sucked in air through her nose and opened her mouth to sigh. David's tongue met hers and gave chase, deepening their kiss.

Mason pulled back, tugging her toward him. Opening her eyes, she could not see beyond David's face as he continued to kiss her. Unsure where to step, she rocked forward more and made contact—contact with David's hard-on as it rested against her. He began mimicking Mason's earlier moves, rubbing against her and rocking her tighter to him each time he pressed forward.

Unsteady and unsure where to step to right herself, Joan rocked backward. David met her partway back and pressed her against Mason. Sandwiched between both, they rocked her feverishly back and forth, whispering their next intentions in each ear.

"Imagine what this would feel like naked." David's voice echoed, briefly breaking through their mutual desire-loaded haze.

"Uhmmm..." Mason's less-than-enthusiastic response brought David's head up from where he nuzzled Joan's neck.

"Can I get some water?" Joan managed to rasp out despite her dry throat.

Mason dropped his hands and turned sideways. "Sure, I'll get it for you." He started to move away when David gripped his hand.

"Why do I feel I'm the only one still in the mood?" He pulled back from Joan, creating a slight space between them.

"Can I sit down before my knees buckle?" Joan grasped David's arm and sat on the bed.

He opened his mouth to speak. Joan shook her head no.

"Hear me out, please." She looked at Mason. "Both of you, okay?"

Taking in their mutual nods, she continued. "I'm not cooling down or wanting to stop. But if we're going to go through with this, I need water and two of these blasted layers gone."

She tugged David's T-shirt off, followed by Mason's. Down to her robe and pajamas, she stood, reaching for the waistband of her velour pants. Looking up, she caught their cat-like stares.

"What is with you two?" She tugged the waist down while keeping her robe from bunching up. Tossing the pants on a chair, she sat back down and crossed her arms.

"If you think I'm stripping more by myself, you're wrong. We are gonna do it together and do it mutually."

She glanced from Mason to David. David's sheepish grin and nod indicated he was in. Turning back to Mason, she found him moving across the room toward the kitchenette. Was he in or out?

"Mason," Joan started, rising and going to him. "Are you okay? It's all right to say what you're feeling."

Mason filled a glass with water and hastily drank. Refilling it, he handed it to her. "Yeah, I'm fine. Like you, the heat has dried my mouth and muddled my thoughts. I think it's time for a bit of truth without the dare and be sure we're all on board before we continue."

David joined them and reached for a glass. "Are you saying you're in on continuing?"

Mason stepped aside and leaned on the counter. "Yes, I'm fine with going on. But I want to be sure we've agreed to it and get our unspoken fears out of the way."

"Why now?" Joan refilled her glass and sat at the table, sipping her water.

David joined her. "Refill your glass and sit down. We've got a discussion going."

Mason chuckled and sat his glass on the table. "I managed to snag a box of Nilla wafers. How about a snack while we talk?"

"I'd like to get in on that." Joan emptied her glass and handed it to Mason. "A little sweet treat to refuel. David?"

"Sure, why not? A hard cock needs its strength."

Mason grabbed the box and joined them at the table.

"You wanna know why I'm talking now and not before?" He opened the box and dumped several cookies on a paper towel.

"Well, yeah, seeing as you seemed to avoid talking to me earlier and acted aloof for the better part of the evening." David popped a cookie into his mouth.

Joan snapped hers in two and bit into half. Laying the remainder on a napkin, she turned to Mason.

"I've gotten mixed signals from you up to the last few minutes. While I'm not privy to what you two," she pointed to David, "have talked about, I think we've each got some concerns we need to air before we go any further."

Mason watched Joan's face, waiting to catch any fleeting signal before glancing at David. Catching both their nods and relaxed postures, he decided to spill his guts.

"I don't want to lose either of you as friends. I care about both of you and don't want to split you up."

David laid his hand on the table. "I understand your concerns. Maybe even fears. I've shared with you before and there's been no problem. Why now?"

Mason started to shrug when Joan took his hand. "Mason, don't hold back. Talk to me. Tell me what's going on in here." She touched his head. "And there." She moved her hand to his chest, close to his heart.

"I agree with her." David rose and placed the closed Nilla wafers box back on the counter. "I know you've mentioned Joan's a hottie more than once since she and I began dating."

Mason swallowed hard and nodded. He'd started this conversation, said he was game to continue and get things out in the open, so how did he get past his fears and jeers?

Joan squeezed his hand and pulled it to her lips. The soft brush of her heated lips over his knuckles made his cock jerk every time his heart throbbed. Christ, how much assurance did he need?

"Mason, spit out what you're keeping bottled up." David patted his shoulder. "I know you think Joan is hot. Sexy hot as you've said several times tonight without saying it directly. Why not admit you want her?"

"I thought I'd already done that." Mason arched an eyebrow and squinted as he looked sideways at David. He wanted to make sure he caught Joan's reaction simultaneously.

Since their conversation and actions had turned candid and intimate, he hoped he wasn't going to botch anything.

Joan smiled and leaned forward, resting her elbows on the table and her chin on her hands. Nodding, she winked at him. "I picked up on your desire as we made out. Are you ready to see it through?"

"Well, experience marks us all. Last time I mentioned even a passing interest in another friend's lady, I got a busted nose, black eye, and lost a longtime best friend. Shit, even looking at another guy's woman with mundane thoughts is frowned upon, much less thinking about her sexually." He diverted his gaze and toyed with his half-eaten cookie. How far had he stuck his foot in it this time?

Joan released his hand and stood. Mason ducked his head and scrunched his shoulders, waiting for her to connect. Maybe if she smacked him, she'd at least let him sleep in the bed rather than on the floor.

Joan leaned over and kissed his cheek. "It took a lot for you to admit that, didn't it?"

Mason glanced from Joan to David. He swallowed hard, took a deep breath, and nodded. His one burning question needed an answer. The answer he needed to hear and be reassured of before he could openly acknowledge what everyone already knew. "What about us? Us as friends? As individual friends?"

Chapter Nine

David gathered their glasses and moved toward the kitchenette. "Joan, why don't you go first? I'm interested in your answer as well."

Joan touched David as he walked by, blowing him a kiss as he glanced at her. "I see no problems. We've been friends for quite a while. It's not like we're still getting to know each other. I've seen the good and bad sides of you both. And you, me. I care for both of you."

David placed their glasses in the sink and turned. "Never mind what prior fools did or what most people think. I'm not upset you find Joan attractive and want to get in her pants. Thanks for the compliment and trusting both of us to share your feelings." David smiled and continued. "Stop worrying, dude. I don't own Joan, and neither does she me. I've already said if she wants to see others, that's cool. I'd rather it be someone I trust and care about."

"I concur with David. Neither of us has promised the other exclusivity. You know, we started out as friends with benefits and are seeing where it goes and grows from there. We've talked about you being an integral part of us." Joan leaned over, wrapped her arms around Mason's shoulders, and hugged him hard. "Stop worrying and enjoy. Thanks for the compliment."

David moved up behind Joan, resting his hand on her shoulder. "Joan, you've got a point. I'd guess we've been avoiding voicing how we feel simply because we're in new territory. I'm comfortable with you and Mason being lovers.

But honestly, if another person I barely knew broached the idea, I'm not so sure I'd tell you go for it.

"Mason," David started, pausing as he checked out Mason's body language. His posture wasn't as rigid as before. David wet his lips and finished his thought. "Our friendship—yours and mine—is solid. I'm happy to share Joan with you. Or have Joan share us."

Mason's gaze caught his. His nostrils flared as he inhaled. He parted his lips as though he wanted to respond. How much reassurance did he need?

Joan reached out and clasped Mason's wrist. "Mason, friendship is not without choices and chances, even risks. I know being vulnerable and open from your past experiences isn't easy. Your friendship with me is just as solid as yours, and David's is."

Mason nodded and moved his shoulders from side to side. He tugged his wrist free from Joan's hand. Words only backed actions so far. Actions did the rest. The time had come to let go of all uncertainty and move forward. "Joan, I want to make you orgasm and pant as I'm deep inside you."

David's loud whistle caught Joan's and his attention. "Buddy, I'm glad you got that off your chest."

Joan grinned, turning to both of them. "I'm up for the challenge if you are." She pointed to him. "Are you?"

Joan tugged at Mason's arm. "I'd like to resume my Mason seat, please." She grinned and winked at him.

David laughed and winked as well. "Lady knows her mind. Remember to give your seat to a lady, Mama always said."

Mason chuckled and pushed back from the table. "Please have a seat." He patted his lap and reached for Joan's hand. "Let me help Madam to her seat."

Joan pulled up her robe and swung her ass at him saucily before plopping down on his lap. "Whoa, easy there!" His cock nudged heavily against the layers separating him from her pajama shorts.

Joan squirmed, enjoying the feel of Mason's cock against her. A deliciously wicked image flashed through her mind making her squirm more and dampening her shorts quite thoroughly.

Her version of a Joan sandwich raised the odds that both guys were going to end up touching each other and get her double-dipped. One of them in her mouth and one of them in her vagina.

Joan rose and brushed her lips over Mason's. "You and I have a French kiss to finish."

"I thought—" She pressed her fingers against Mason's lips. "Ssssh. David's turn."

Joan turned to David. Crooking her finger, she motioned him to come to her. "You and I have a kiss to finish, too."

David snuck a quick glance at Mason. His hands rose as he shrugged. "Dude, don't let your cock get soft for lack of attention. Thinking about you keeping yourself hot and ready to pleasure Joan turns me on." He grinned and rose. "Damn, maybe I'm an exhibitionist."

Joan's throaty laugh and once-over gaze spoke more than words where her thoughts centered. "Ah, so two hard cocks ready to take you turns you on?"

She nodded, her eyes glowing.

David moved around the table, and Mason, stepping closer to her. "You want a mutual strip—"

David raised his arms. "Your pleasure awaits."

Joan reached out and grabbed the hem of his first shirt.

"Easy on the uniform." He closed the space between them. "One piece at a time."

Licking his lips, he leaned down and pressed his lips to hers.

His shirt tightened around him. Joan must have more clenched in her hands.

"Hey, I need this later," he murmured, his lips still on hers. He slid his hands between them, sliding toward hers. "Help me take it off."

David pulled back. Her gaze matched his. Neither broke eye contact as he slowly freed the shirt from her hands.

Covering her hands with his, he worked them up the front of the shirt toward the collar. "Maybe Mason should join us."

David glanced to where Mason sat, confirming his interest.

Mason swallowed hard and met David's gaze. Watching him and Joan was hot. Hotter than he expected. David's smile and nod toward Joan punctuated his statement.

Mason scooted the chair away from the table and rose. "A mutual strip hot stuff."

He sidestepped David and moved around Joan, pressing close to her side. "How can I help?" He leaned down and nipped her neck.

Joan arched her neck, and a low moan escaped her lips.

"Shall I help you with your robe?' Mason slipped his hand over Joan's wrist, lightly trailing his fingers across the inside of her wrist.

"How about you help her with my shirt? She seems to be all thumbs."

David hunched one shoulder, then his other. "These tight sleeves are hampering our progress."

Mason paused as he carefully searched Joan and David's faces. Neither appeared hesitant. Joan grinned and kissed him. David shrugged and spoke. "Anytime, dude. These sleeves are tight."

Mason kissed Joan and touched David's shoulder. "Sure it isn't your swelled ego or too much steam heat?"

David's snort and grin eased Mason's apprehensions. Sharing two women at the same time or in the same bed differed from one woman taking on each of them separately as they lay close by each other. A lot more touching up close and together made sense and peaked his curious voyeur side, given David's earlier comment. Besides, he agreed with David; seeing Joan pleasured by someone he and she cared about added to the experience.

Moving behind David, he placed his hands near Joan's.

"All right, you move with me on the count of three. One—"

"Three," David blurted out.

All three burst out laughing.

Several minutes later, both men, down to their underwear, sandwiched back between them.

"Damn, you two shuck clothes faster than my kid brother's toddler." Joan gasped as David pulled her to him, unbuttoning two of her robe's six buttons.

"And your gripe is?" David's hot breath feathered down her neck into the open *V* of her robe.

"Yes," Mason said, working his hands inside the robe's collar, rubbing her shoulders. "Just because we made it a show for you, you want to complain?"

His words warmed her neck and worked their way down her back.

"No," she managed to whisper, wondering how much more she could take.

Watching them take turns slowly stripping made her wet and hot.

David's challenge to toss and reveal and Mason's acceptance had sent warm ripples up and down her spine, their overflow steaming her desire to higher levels. How much wetter could she get?

"So now it's our turn to assist you," David hotly whispered in her left ear. His hands worked another button open.

"I do believe you're too dressed for what we have in mind," Mason's voice purred in her right ear.

Joan reminded herself to breathe and tried to inhale deeply.

"Cat got your tongue?" David quipped and leaned closer.

Mason's hands mimicked David's moves, massaging across her neck and shoulders in unison.

Lips and tongues captured various parts of her exposed neck and ears. A hand moved lower, stroking the top of her breast, and roamed back toward her shoulder. Another worked the three remaining buttons of her robe open.

She couldn't tell whose hands were whose unless she opened her eyes and attempted to look. Not that she could. Desire kept her tightly wrapped in its embrace. She really didn't care who touched her where and stoked her molten core closer to eruption.

"Oh yes. So beautiful." David's voice whispered across her cheek and partway up her ear. His voice ebbed and flowed almost in rhythm to his caresses.

A set of hands worked her loose robe off her shoulders and down her arms. Lips feathered kisses across her exposed neck, stopping at the collar of her pajama top. Wet licks and flicks of a tongue traced the outer edge of the exposed flesh. Hands stroked down the tops of her breasts, edging closer to her tightly pebbled nipples. How much hotter and tighter could they

get? It was like her heart and clit connected her pulse points. She swore they thrummed each time the guys touched her.

"God, so soft and tasty." Mason nibbled along Joan's shoulder, moving toward her arm. Each nip and kiss brought her top closer to sliding off as David and Mason unbuttoned her top.

David slipped his hand inside her top, bunching it against his wrist the higher he stroked. The heat of his palm scalded its way along her stomach, moving upward. He slid his other around her waist and pulled her tighter to him. Grabbing her top in both hands, David pulled it open, exposing her breasts. "Too much clothing and so little exposure."

Mason raised his head. His warm breath caressed Joan's shoulder. "Oh, I like this view!"

He took her hand and raised it to his shoulder. "Hold on, sweetie. I think a southern reveal is needed." He trailed his fingertips over her stomach, tracing a path around her navel and inched toward her waistband. As he reached the edge of her shorts, he worked two fingers under the elastic and snaked his palm below her navel, stopping short of her mons.

He felt Joan's sharp inhale as she gripped his shoulder. "Like that, do you?" Dragging his nails along the edge of her hairline, he leaned closer. "Wait until my tongue gets there."

David tweaked and pulled her nipple between strokes of his other hand up and down her bare back. Currents of sweet need rippled down her chest and straight to her core. Mason's touch and innuendos added fuel to her growing desire. How much more could she take and not orgasm from sheer anticipation?

"God, yes, I love what you're doing. Both of you." Joan tried to turn her head toward David. A need to kiss him and feel his heat built up in her. Then Mason and back to cradled between them both. She wanted them naked. Every stitch of clothing gone, eliminated and nothing between them.

"Naked. I need to be naked. It's so hot and sweet." As Mason worked his fingers between her legs, a low moan began deep in her throat. Two more strokes and her clit—

"Ye–ss–ss." His fingers hit pay dirt. Her clit thrummed with each swipe. "Much more, and I'm going to orgasm. I'm so wet."

"That's no problem if you want me to stop." Mason began pulling his hand out of her panties.

Joan dropped her hand from Mason's shoulder and grabbed his arm. "Don't stop. Not yet." Her gaze met his.

Chapter Ten

"Who am I to deny the lady her wish?" Mason worked his fingers back over Joan's clit, circling it twice before pinching the nub between his fingers and mimicking David's movements on her nipple.

"David, a kiss, please. Share my orgasm with me." Joan panted and puckered her lips.

"I can't deny the lady either." David turned sideways, anchoring Joan against him, capturing her lips with his.

"Oh, what a sweet cream this is going to be." Mason stroked firmer, nudging his fingers lower between her legs.

"Hmmm," Joan groaned as David broke off their kiss. "Ye—ss do no—tt stop."

David wrapped his arms around Joan's waist. "Let go, sweetie. Go for it."

Joan nodded, inhaled, and cried out. "So good. Oh my god. Mason, that is so good." More moans and ahs sounded until Joan leaned limply against David.

David tucked her hair behind her ears, getting it out off her face. He kissed her cheek and winked at Mason. "Good job, my friend. I think the lady approves."

Joan's weak *uh-huh* brought a smile to both men's faces.

"I don't think I could move if I wanted to." Joan sighed and started fanning herself.

"I think I can assist with that." David straightened Joan upright against him. He moved backward, Mason moved with them—his hand still in Joan's panties, until David felt the bed touching his legs.

Easing Joan off him, he held her loosely in the bend of one arm. "Mason, how about we strip the lady and cool her off a bit?"

Mason's grin and exuberant nod were contagious. David chuckled. "Eagerness is not vastly overrated, eh, my friend?"

"No, not at all. You take the top? I'll take the bottom." Mason worked his hand free and stepped back.

David grasped Joan's hand and helped her sit on the bed. "Are you ready for the next phase?" He leaned down and brushed his lips over hers. "I think it's time to work on your earlier suggestion. Get you naked." David drew out the word *naked* before tugging Joan's arm upward.

"Off with this offending piece of clothing." He worked her arm through the sleeve of her top. Leaning across her, he raised her other arm and glanced at Mason. "I was going to ask for your help. But I see you're busy."

Mason's boxers hung low on his hips. His cock stuck out over the top, peeking out of his fist as he stroked downward. "Never let a good scene go to waste, I say."

David let go of Joan's arm and stood. Moving between Mason and Joan, he worked her other arm free of her top. Reaching back, he tapped Mason on the hip. "Watch where you're stroking, dude. Don't want to wear that thing out."

Mason snorted and offered a cheesy comeback. "Haven't yet and doubt I will before the night's over."

David tossed Joan's top on the chair with her robe. Turning around, he caught Mason's glazed look. "Hey, waste not, want not. You ready to take this off, Joan?" David snapped the elastic of her shorts, getting both their attentions.

"Ouch! That smarts." Joan cuffed him on the arm. "I'm a participant in this, too."

Mason slipped his hand down to his balls and released his cock. He leaned forward and kissed Joan. "Wanna help clean up my fingers?" He pressed two fingers against Joan's lips. She opened and laved her tongue across the bottom of them. Mason thrust them in and out as she puckered her lips around them.

"Damn, that is hot. I want to feel your hot, greedy mouth milking me dry, babe." Mason shook his hips, swinging his cock back and forth. "Arrgh, got to get those shorts off you and your legs over my shoulders. You're gonna cream another sweet taste for me. Aren't ya?"

Joan shivered and ducked her head. She looked up, trying to act coy by peering through her lashes. She caught Mason's grin and him shaking his finger at her.

"Shame, shame. You wanton thing. You know that is gonna cost you. Maybe I'll make you orgasm twice or three times before I let you taste this." Mason grabbed his boxers and shoved them down his hips. His cock stuck out, hard and beautiful. Even his balls seemed to swell as she gazed at them. Wetting her lips, Joan reached out.

"Oh, no. You have to wait. These come off first." Mason pointed to her shorts and worked his boxers the rest of the way off.

Joan began to stand. Mason snickered. "I'm taking them off. You lay back and spread those lovely legs." Mason moved forward. He caught David eyeing their interaction as he fondled his cock. "See, you've got him hotter, too."

David stood and stripped off his shorts. "I'm going to enjoy the show." He moved to the head of the bed and propped up two pillows. "Go ahead and play at will."

Lying back against the pillows, he squeezed the end of his cock, urging more pre-cum out. As he coated his cock, David spread his legs, easing his bloated balls into a more comfortable position.

Mason eased Joan onto the bed. He quickly glanced at David. His wink and brief nod indicated no harm or foul done. Taking two quick breaths, Mason knelt on the floor. "Lay back and enjoy."

Joan leaned back on her hands, keeping her upper half where she could see both. She reached back with one hand and touched David. A quick reassuring rub, she tilted her head back to make sure he was all right. She noted his airborne kiss and smile before he settled back into the pillows at his back. Easing down, she snapped her fingers at Mason and spoke. "I don't think you're up to your own challenge."

Mason chose to ignore Joan's taunt and worked one hand under her hip and buttocks. He pinched and fondled her firm ass before easing one leg over his shoulder. Leaning forward, he puckered his lips and blew.

Joan squirmed, raising her hips as she tried to wriggle away. Mason caught her ankle as she attempted to regain footing on the bed. "Nope, you don't get away from me that easily."

He quickly worked her other leg over his shoulder. Placing both hands on her hips, he spoke. "Now I'll see who is up to the challenge."

He peeled her pink, lush nether lips open, exposing her plump clitoris. Two dewy drops of wetness lay atop the prize as if waiting to be lapped up. Mason blew over the wet, exposed flesh, moving back and forth, leaving no area untouched. Joan's throaty groan and low *uhhh* told him he'd succeeded in pushing her heat higher.

Joan jerked as he flicked his tongue lightly near her clit. Raising his head, he watched as she clenched the bedspread in both hands. David's smile and quick strokes told Mason he'd lit a fire that wouldn't soon go out.

"Don't worry about me." David scooted closer. "I've got the best view." He leaned down and tweaked Joan's nipple. Her sharp hiss and twitch told both men they had her stirred up and sizzling. David gave Mason a thumbs-up as he glanced up from Joan's mons.

Mason inched higher, positioning himself tight to Joan. He inhaled her aroma with each breath. She smelled as good as she tasted. Her mock challenge egged him on, yet he knew if he went too fast, David wouldn't have a chance to also bring her off. This was going to take teamwork. No one liked bad sex or lousy lovers. Sometimes it couldn't be helped. Mason was going to be damn sure that didn't happen. "Wanna make sure the lady gets what she needs with us. A few suggestions here and there are welcomed."

Mason blew one more time over Joan's swollen clit. She jerked toward him. Sticking his tongue out, he dove in. Hot, taut flesh slid under his tongue, coating the underside with one exotic taste. He lapped upward, teasing the underneath of her nub briefly before reaching the top. One swipe, two, and then three fast. Joan rocked against him, panting and moaning with each lick.

"Yes, that is so good." She arched her neck, rocking her head back with each thrust of her hips against his face and questing tongue.

David stroked down and up his cock three times rapidly and let go. Mason gave as good as he got. Joan hadn't stopped squirming since he'd buried his face between her legs. "Let's see what I can do to up the ante."

David licked his thumb and forefinger on each hand. Positioning himself near Joan's shoulder, he leaned forward. On her next thrash, he plucked her tight nipples with his fingers and rolled them, pulling forward as she lay back.

He squeezed Joan's nipples harder and worked them up and back like two corkscrews. Watching her face begin to flush and her rapid thrusts against Mason, David knew she was close. Close to creaming all over Mason's face and lips. She'd challenged him. Mason wasn't going to lose if David could help it. "Suckle her between your lips and flick your tongue as fast as you can."

David caught Mason's nod as Joan contorted between them.

"N–o–o–o faa–iirrr," Joan chanted. Her mouth hung open as she arched her back and tried to lift her hips off the bed. "I'm—I'm going to—"

With every lap of his tongue, Mason felt Joan's clit throb. It swelled and pulsated every time he flicked at her. She was too close to hold back. Loosening his hold on her hips, he slid both hands under her buttocks and raised her tight against him. Letting go of her clit, he slipped lower and thrust his tongue into her, flicking as fast as he could.

Joan's short yelp and gasp caught David's attention. "Easy, love, let it take you where you want to go."

Joan gripped his wrist and held on. He knew the signal. Pain no longer felt exquisite or added pleasure. David let go of Joan's nipples and moved back against the pillows.

"Oh man, I yield, Mason," Joan managed to rasp out as she dropped back to the mattress. "You're damn good."

Mason pushed back against the bed, leveraging himself upright. Taking part of the sheet, he wiped his face. "Thanks. Glad you enjoyed it." He sat on the bed close to Joan and reached out, taking her hand in his. "What's next?"

Joan struggled to sit up. Mason helped her move to the end of the bed and sit up. "I'm game for round two. Who calls it this time? David or me?" She turned toward David and licked her lips.

David sat with his eyes partially closed, fondling his balls. He stroked up very slowly toward the top of his cock and then rapidly returned to where his other hand cupped his balls. His nipples pebbled, sticking out like fine-point pen tips. His sharp inhalations and groans indicated he was close to his own release.

"I'd say David gets to call it. He's working up to a hot, delicious orgasm." Mason stood up. He retrieved the box of condoms they'd purchased earlier from the bag hanging on the closet doorknob.

Tossing the box on the bed, Mason offered his hand to Joan. "I'm wanting more group participation this round. How about you?"

Joan took Mason's hand and yanked. "Come here, and let's see if we can distract David."

She caught Mason as he fell toward her. "Easy there. I want to bring both of you off at the same time. How do we go about doing this?"

Joan faced David. His hands held his cock midway down his shaft. His eyes flicked back and forth from her to Mason. His lustful look said his mind was cooking up something. "I know that look. He's got a plan, and his vivid imagination is working overtime. I think we best hear him out and get it going real time."

Mason's snort and smirk, along with David's enthusiastic nod, sent warm ripples rushing down her neck and chest. The effect cooled her back to simmering. Joan stretched out prone, facing both, and pulled the box of condoms to her. "Okay, spill it. What, or who, am I doing next and how?"

Chapter Eleven

David sat up and scooted to the edge of the mattress. "Give me a condom and on your knees."

Mason reached for the condoms. Joan shook her head, tightening her grip on the box.

David winked at Mason."Trade places with me, and let's see how compliant our lady decides to be."

Mason sidestepped David, letting him by.

Joan lay still on the bed, clutching the box of condoms, watching their movement. "Do you honestly think I'm not paying attention? Can't hear what you're saying?"

"She speaks. Maybe she'll participate and stop grasping the box like a neon sign." Mason winked and took David's previous spot lounging at the head of the bed. David pulled Joan toward him.

Joan tried to lurch away. The slickness of the spread and the bunching of the sheets offered no help, only hindrance, leaving her sprawled on the bed, ass in the air.

David tugged her gently a few inches before letting go. He moved to where he could clearly see her, and she him. Her breasts stuck out as Joan began to prop herself up, seeking leverage to move. David waited until her elbows touched the mattress at the same time her knees did. He brought his hand back and swung forward. Joan scrambled to move before his hand

could connect with her ass again. The box slipped out of her hands as she pushed against the sheets attempting to scoot backward.

Mason leaned forward, tugged the top sheet toward him, and popped the box into the air. It landed close to him. He picked it up as Joan reached the end of the bed closest to David. "Why are you so flustered?"

Joan worked herself off the bed, turning to face David. "I'm not flustered. I'm thinking about how to get you both off at the same time."

"About the same, maybe rapid. The idea of all of us orgasming together is intriguing." Mason smirked and glanced at Joan. "What you got in mind?"

Joan sat on the bed, eyeing David and Mason. Feigning a yawn, she batted her eyelashes at them and gave a plucky grin. "Well, depends on how interested you both are."

David's chuckle and Mason's snort told her they weren't buying her tired approach. "Okay, okay. I want one of you in my vagina and one in my mouth. There, satisfied?"

"No, not yet, but soon." David dragged out *soon*. Mason rubbed his hands together gleefully and kept nodding.

She pointed at David. "Mutual consent all around, okay? Mason, you get to say what you want first. Then David."

Mason blew Joan an airborne kiss and touched his lips. "I want to feel your luscious, hot mouth all around me, babe. I'll consider luxuriating in your hot wetness if we're still up to it."

Joan nodded and ducked her head. Mason could almost feel the heat rising from her and filling the room. The last time he and David had shared a threesome this hot, both of them slept soundly for eight hours in blissed-out repose with a hot mama between them. Mason suspected their mutual blowouts would knock them out if the heat rose much more. Or leave them high, dry, and blissed out for the night. "David, you in?"

David sat down and leaned to grab the box of condoms. "Yes, I am. I'll light her fire and put it out. Joint fireworks and joint bliss. Look out and hope we don't set the smoke detector off."

He ripped open the box, pulling out two condoms. "Joan, you going down with or without one?" He held up a foil packet. "I trust Mason and know he's clean. The choice is yours, though."

Joan glanced at him and then at Mason. "Thanks for trusting me and allowing me to make my own decision. I'm clean, too, and I know you are, David. Mason, anything to disclose?"

Mason looked at him, then at Joan. "No, I'm clean, too. Last tests were two months ago. All good."

Joan touched David's hand. "I don't need that. I want to taste Mason *au naturel*."

David pushed the box aside and rose. "Joan, what is easier for you to reach Mason? Go ahead and get comfortable. I'll join you in a moment."

Joan scooted close to Mason, positioning herself next to his splayed legs. "Why not let me taste you as well first? Get you ready to put that on unless you want my help."

David swallowed hard, fumbling with the foil packet as he tried to open it. The packet slipped out of his hand, flipping through the air and landing next to Joan. Mason's chuckle, followed by Joan's laugh, tugged at David's heart. His girl and his best friend, two of the most important people in his world, weren't backing away.

"Guess I'm all thumbs?" David shrugged and leaned forward to retrieve the packet.

"Let me." Joan picked up the foil and tore it open, easing the condom into her hand. "Ease back onto the bed, and let's see what some TLC does for you and this?" Joan fondled his cock with her free hand.

David worked his way up the bed until he lay near Joan. He caught Mason's quick grin and thumbs-up signal. Joan rose on her knees between them. Her smile and bright eyes said more than words. Each of them was ready for where things went from here.

Joan scooted over to Mason, touching and fondling him before moving over to David. Threading her hand into his hair, she pulled him toward her capturing his lips with hers.

Slowly she traced his mouth, stopping to brush her lips over his. She nibbled his chin before nipping his throat near his chest. "Hmmm, you taste good."

Palming the condom in her other hand, she trailed her fingers down his chest and around each hard nipple. "Ooh, you're excited. That makes me hot." Joan leaned forward, worrying the closest one to her with her teeth and lips. David's sharp hiss and jerk said she'd gotten to him.

Leaning further across him, Joan gave his other nipple equal treatment. "Just like the two of you are doing to me. Pain and pleasure. So close to each other." She licked a fingertip and rimmed his areola. Watching David's stuttered breathing, she knew going lower and lapping his navel would get his cock hard, ready for some hot nips and laps.

Joan rose on her hands and knees, working her way down David's side, brushing her lips and tongue against him. She laved and blew on the wet trail she made as she got closer to his cock. Working backward toward the edge of his groin, she sucked and nipped bits of flesh, leaving slight bite marks every few inches. David's soft groans told her he was turned on and getting hotter the lower she moved with each swipe of her tongue.

"Damn, Joan, that is sweet. So hot and sweet," David groaned. His hips jerked, sending his cock bobbing toward her as though it silently pleaded with her. *Come on and kiss me.*

"Poor baby," Joan whispered against David's stomach, slowly scratching her nails along the top edge of his pubic hair. "I bet you need some cooling off like this."

Joan grasped the base of David's cock, puckering her lips, and kissed his cockhead on all sides. Opening her mouth, Joan drew him in, tightening her mouth around him as he thrust forward. She flicked her tongue over and around his tip, wetting it thoroughly.

"Oh, yes," David moaned, rocking his hips forward, working himself in and out of her mouth. "That is so damn good."

Joan slid her mouth up and down his shaft, moistening every part. Easing him out of her mouth, Joan laid the condom on David's belly and slipped her hand between his legs. Gently cupping his balls, she fondled them briefly. Their weight and warmth spoke volumes of David's excitement. Hotter than his cock and heavy with the need to orgasm, she leaned down and licked them. "Don't worry, my poor darlings. Release is coming."

Joan pulled up, took one more swipe with her tongue over David's cockhead and palmed the condom. "Think you can stand my handling you a bit longer to encase you and move to the next level of pleasure?"

David gripped handfuls of the bedspread, willing himself to breathe deeper and speak. Two short inhalations and one heavy out. He licked his lips and spoke. "Don't be too long about it. I'm edging close and want to enjoy being in you, letting it soak before I bring you and me off."

Joan's quick smile and nod said she knew how touchy he'd gotten. As much as he'd love to bury his cock deep inside her, he wasn't sure how much control he'd have to ensure her pleasure.

"How about you let me put this on?" He worked the condom out of Joan's hand. "You get Mason ready to enjoy more than a show. I'll join you in a bit."

Joan grinned and blew David a kiss. "Sounds good to me."

David touched her arm. "Hon, I'm too close to have much control left and ease into you slowly. I need to feel your heat around me. I want to share your orgasm with you. Feel you coat me with your pleasure. Okay?"

Joan ducked her head and glanced toward Mason. "I'm sure all of us are ready to rock ourselves to a blissed-out state. What do you say, Mason?"

Mason grunted. He squeezed his cockhead again and fondled his balls. Pain and pleasure mixed so well, but the fine edge walked by both could blow things out of control if not handled carefully. "I'd love to watch David take you to a mind-blowing orgasm. I know I'll be enjoying your hot lips and mouth churning up mine."

Joan grinned and brushed her lips across David's and then Mason's. "I'm doubly blessed. Two caring lovers."

Joan turned on her hands and knees so she faced David, allowing him to touch and finger her until he was ready to enter her. Glancing between her legs, she watched as he began working the condom down and over his cock. His cock stood almost straight up and barely quivered as he rolled the condom down the shaft. Last time she'd seen him this hard, he'd almost orgasmed from rubbing against her. She wasn't sure how long any of them would last once they began.

A hand threaded through her hair, tugging backward slightly. Joan looked up. Mason's tight grip on his cock said he was close, too. "You need me to help put that on cool-down?" She reached out and fondled Mason's balls.

"Easssy," Mason hissed through clenched teeth. "Right now, pain or pleasure is going to send me spurting. I'd rather feel you bringing me there than doing it myself." He eased his hand off his cock and lifted his pre-cum-coated fingers to Joan's mouth. "Care for a taste before the main course?" He pressed against her lips.

Joan's tongue slipped up and down his palm and laved his fingers before she suckled two into her mouth, nipping at his fingertips as he worked them in and out. "Eager and ready, I see."

Joan slurped his fingers in one last time and released them. "I like the taste, but the appetizer wasn't enough. More, please." Her grin and dip of her head toward his cock urged him forward.

Mason stuffed two more pillows behind him and slid lower on the bed. "Hope this makes things easier for you." He spread his legs apart and tucked his hands behind his head. "Go for it. I'm all yours."

Chapter Twelve

Mason watched David kneel on the bed, using Joan's hips to steady him. Moving slowly across the mattress, he stopped close to her. His quirky grin said his ironic sense of humor had taken flight. "Thank God we aren't on a blasted water bed, or we'd all be green from the motion."

Mason snorted. "That's for sure."

Joan chuckled. Her warm breath oozed over Mason's cock. Much more, and he'd ejaculate as soon as she took him in. Her words indicated he didn't have long to wait. "Since we don't have to worry, I'm enjoying my main course."

"Oh, sweet heaven. Yes!" Mason jerked his hips partly off the mattress. The heat of Joan's mouth engulfed him. She lapped the tip of her tongue around in circles before easing more of him deeper into her mouth. "Ah-aah. So good...I'm going to shoot from my balls on this one." Mason arched his back and squinted.

David eased two fingers into Joan's hot sheath and thrust. Her wetness flowed over his fingers and lubed part of his palm. Turning his hand sideways, he found her clit and began rubbing in short and tight circles across her swollen crest. Her throaty *uhhmmm* and backward thrust said more than if she'd spoken.

"Yes, love. Enjoy." David worked his fingers in and out, stroking Joan's clit in between. Mason's eyes narrowed as her head began bobbing in earnest.

David snuggled tight to her and pressed home, guiding his cock deep into her. "Wet, hot, and—aah." He gasped and grabbed her hips, holding her tight to him.

Spasm after spasm squeezed him, bringing him closer to the edge. Joan could orgasm several times before she hit her hard, bliss-causing one. David slowly eased back, rubbing against her G-spot before sliding almost all the way out. He waited as her wetness washed over him, lubricating the condom and him.

"Slow down, love," David whispered, leaning forward and nipping her shoulder. "I want us to orgasm together. Let's try and keep up with each other."

Mason twisted the bedspread bunched in his hands left and right. "I don't know how much longer...I–I–I can last." He panted and shook his head. "This is so damn good. Better than my fantasies ever were or could be."

Joan arched her back as David nipped closer to her neck and pushed back into her. Heat and need coiled tighter and deeper in her belly. Mason's hands dropped the bedspread and clutched her head, holding her steady as he thrust with faster and shorter strokes in and out of her mouth. As if David could read and feel the rhythm, he quickened his pace, working his thrusts counter to Mason's.

Joan could feel Mason getting harder and warmer with each thrust. His hips jerked upward, and remained off the bed. His balls tapped her chin with each shudder. Keeping suction as steady as she could, she pulled back, slackening off on how much of Mason she took. She bobbed down and released him. "Signal when you are ready to blow. I will swallow but need to know so I don't choke." She reached for him, ready to tuck him back into her mouth.

"Not yet." Mason covered his cock. "I want to watch David work you into a frenzy. See you orgasm once before I do." He slipped his hand up and down his shaft before returning to the head and squeezing. "Oh, yes. I can last a bit longer."

Joan nodded and tightened as she rocked back and forth, trying to keep pace with David. Desire roared up out of her belly and erupted like a volcanic explosion, taking her deep into its grip. Her eyes closed, and she leaned forward, crooning as wave after wave of pleasure rippled through her. "Another, please," she managed to spit out.

"Damn, that is beautiful," Mason moaned. Joan looked up and caught his gaze along with his hand, slowly caressing his shaft in an upward stroke, stopping below the head as though he teased himself. His hot, eye-humping stare made her throat go dry. His eyes raked over her, up and down as though he memorized and touched every part of her.

Rising up on her hands, Joan glimpsed back at David, also seeing his heat gaze focused on her. Searing tendrils of wanton need exploded deep in her, increasing as she glanced from Mason to David and back. One more delicious orgasm, and she was down. Down for the count and out. Sleep and bliss demanded satisfaction as well.

Joan reached out with one hand, motioning Mason closer. "I need to taste and feel you throb as I bring you off." She licked her lips and leaned toward him.

David clasped Joan's hips, steadying himself each time she moved. Each flex and pull of her tugged him closer to his release. "Easy on the moves. I'm not too far behind ya. Ease us over to Mason, and let's take this to the intense level."

Joan pushed back against him, tightening her muscles as she did. David groaned, closed his eyes, and gripped her harder. "Keep that up, and I will shoot right now."

"Hang on. I'm moving," Mason said. David opened his eyes. Mason had scooted next to Joan and was working to position his cock closer to her mouth.

Mason slid one leg between Joan's arms. If he moved closer to her and got her right over his cock, she'd straddle him. Reaching behind him, Mason pulled a pillow on top of him. "Can you work this beneath me so I'm about mouth-level, and you can't miss me?" He winked as he raised his hips and began stuffing the pillow under him.

"I'm not sure how much I can help. But keep pumping your ass up and down like that, and maybe I'll just slurp you in and out." Joan giggled and used her free hand to push the pillow under Mason on his next hump. Tossing her head, she moved her hair out of the way. She noticed Mason pausing. Not bothering to ask why he paused, Joan leaned down and sucked him into her mouth.

"Oh, sweet Jesus. Woman, if your vagina is as tight as your mouth, David and I are gonna blow and be done." Mason pumped his cock rapidly in and out of her puckered lips. Panting, he lowered his hips to the pillow and heaved a deep sigh.

David leaned over Joan and slipped his hand around her waist. He traced her mons, working toward her vagina. If they all orgasmed together, each would feed and fuel their release off the others. Pacing was important. "Slack your legs a bit, babe. Let me find your clit and bring you to a double orgasm with us."

Joan eased her legs open, allowing David to find her clit. "I'm not sure you can reach what you need to do that." She shook her ass against him.

David groaned and pulled back some. He made sure he stayed buried in her heat. He ground his hips counterclockwise and back, pausing long enough to sink deeper into her before easing back out to the point of almost withdrawing. "Play with fire, and you get hot steam happening."

David slipped out and rubbed his hands up and down the small of Joan's back. "How about you lie on your side and let me take you that way so you can lick Mason from his balls to his cockhead without choking as I work you to a double blow?"

Mason grunted as Joan engulfed all of him down to his balls and sucked hard. "Keep that up, and I will drain my balls dry now." Threading his fingers into her hair, he tugged and tried to scoot away. "I want you to enjoy what we're doing so much that you ask for a repeat performance again and again."

Joan popped Mason out of her mouth and grasped the base of his cock. "I'm already planning the next feat. For now, let's get comfortable and cause one hell of an explosion."

Joan slid her legs out behind her, rolling onto one hip. She raised her top leg in the air and glanced at David. He knelt on the bed, stroking his condom-covered cock. Dampness glistened on the latex sheath announcing how turned on she was.

"Looks like that needs more of this." She placed two fingers deep into herself and rubbed her G-spot until shivers erupted, taking her closer to what they sought. Drawing her fingers out, she traced her clit, moaning and jerking with each pass. "Oh, my god, that is so good. I'm ready for us to orgasm together."

David straddled Joan's lower leg and eased back inside her. Joan balanced her raised leg against David's shoulder. "At this angle, my clit and G-spot are throbbing. It feels like you're

deeper and further in me than before." Joan rocked from side to side, moaning as David used a counter rhythm to stay joined with her.

Mason maneuvered his way around Joan, getting to where he could see what was happening while remaining close to her. "Damn, that looks hot. You're deep inside her for sure."

David nodded and thrust fast into Joan, eliciting a deep moan from her. "Yes, this position allows deep penetration, and I can get her clit, too. Double hard blow, and she loves it."

Joan took hold of Mason and hissed, "It's not nice to talk with your mouth full. I'm ready to enjoy your whipped cream." She puckered her lips and deep-throated Mason.

"Ah–hh she is hot. Come on in, David. Join the fray, and let's erupt together." Mason worked his hips back and forth, pumping in and out of Joan's mouth.

David eased Joan's leg around his waist and leaned into the *V* of her legs. Slicking his fingers with her juices, he stroked between her labia and found her clit. Swollen, plump, and twitching, he knew she was close. Making sure to not to stroke to close to the tip of the nub, he feathered caresses around the pearl and teased up to the sensitive edges of it poking out of its hood. He eased out, pulling every inch of him slowly across her G-spot, to the point of withdrawing. David watched as Joan began bobbing her head faster and cupping Mason's balls.

Mason's eyes drooped halfway closed, indicating he wasn't far off.

David eased into Joan and tweaked her clit. She jerked and pushed firmer against him. Two fast strokes of his thumb over her clit and a couple of semi-thrusts had her rocking back against him. Her tight sheath got wetter and began tightening around him. "Yes, babe. I'm there."

David clenched his teeth and rapidly thrust in and out. Leaning over Joan, he took her pebbled nipple in his hand and twisted. Her muffled grunt and moan said she was not far behind him. Ripple after ripple of muscle washed over him as her wetness increased. He could feel her G-spot pulse with each ripple.

Mason raised his hips and pushed into Joan's open mouth. He clenched hands full of the bedspread and closed his eyes. Pulse after pulse of hard-core pleasure raced down his cock straight to his balls, pulling them tighter against him. If Joan sucked him down to them again and kept flicking her tongue over him, he'd—"Oh yeah! Oh I am there!"

Mason arched his back and went still. Slowly, he began dropping to the bed.

David picked up speed, circling his hips as he ground against Joan. Joan tightened around him as her orgasm increased in intensity. He pushed in and quickly rubbed her clit. Keeping his strokes short and tight, David pumped in Joan twice as shots of pleasure streamed over him and enveloped his balls. It grew in strength each time Joan's clit throbbed. "One more time, and I'm there too. Ahhh, God, that's good!"

Chapter Thirteen

David caught himself on his elbows as he began to collapse, with the last surge of his orgasm rushing over him. Checking on Joan, he caught her glassy-eyed gaze and stifled yawn. Her quick nod and airborne kiss told him she was all right. Easing back, he encircled his cock with his thumb and forefinger, ensuring he kept the condom on as he withdrew. He worked his way to the edge of the bed and stood.

Mason laid spread-eagle on the bed. His cock lay against his leg, streaks of jisim coating parts of him. David grinned as Mason cracked open one eye and stuck out his tongue. "Pppfffft. Yeah, it still works."

Joan snickered. David snorted. "I think we all could use one last drink of water, and then I'm calling dibs on the side of the bed closest to the bathroom."

Mason sat up and scooted to the end of the bed. He leaned over and kissed Joan's stomach before he stood.

"Eeek. That tickles. Behave, Mason." Joan reached up and stroked his cheek. "I'm with David. I need to brush my teeth and use the bathroom. Then I'm out. I'm so sleepy." She tried to stifle a yawn behind her hand. "Good sex and bliss are great sleep inducers."

Mason patted Joan's thigh and walked into the kitchenette. "I'm gonna use the sink here to brush my teeth and wash up. Anyone else calling dibs on bed spots?" He turned and winked at Joan.

Joan rose and walked past Mason smacking him on the ass. "I'm taking the middle. That way I get covers and warmth from you two. Now where is my T-shirt?"

"Here, use mine." David tossed his to her. "I'm rinsing off in the shower. Anyone else think that's better than using a sink and washcloth?" He pointed to Mason and trotted toward the bathroom door.

"Hey, no fair," Mason called out, trying to edge past David. "You won't leave any warm water."

Joan stepped around them, grabbing her makeup case off the counter. "When you two decide who's next, let me know. I'm going first."

Twenty minutes later, they crawled into bed and pulled the blankets over themselves. Joan lay nestled between Mason and David. Each had kissed her goodnight and felt her up before turning on their sides, promising not to snore too loudly. Joan couldn't help smiling and humming softly. What had started out as an odd, off-the-wall incident hadn't turned out too badly. Where did they go from here? She blinked her eyes and inhaled. Slowly counting to five, she exhaled. Sleep overcame her and scrambled her last thoughts.

Ten hours later

Mason squinted one eye open. Sunlight showed around the blackout curtains covering the window. He remembered looking at his watch before David turned off the bedside lamp. They'd pulled the covers over them shortly before one a.m. How long had they slept?

Easing onto his back, Mason worked his arms out from under the top sheet. David's soft snores indicated he was still asleep. Mason smiled as Joan snuggled closer, resting her hand on his chest. Once during the night, she'd spooned to him, murmuring she was cold. Holding her, her bare buttocks tucked tightly against his groin, her T-shirt-covered breasts touching him had sent his mind wandering down paths previously only fantasized about. In the light of day, reality set in.

Was last night a fluke? A one-time occurrence? What repercussions were any of them facing?

A loud knock sounded. Its staccato noise woke David and Joan.

"Stay put. I'll get it." Mason tossed back the sheet and rose. His morning hard-on drew Joan's smile. He shook his hips briefly from side to side.

The knock sounded again. Louder than the first time.

"One moment," Mason called out, hurrying across the room, grabbing his shorts and a nearby shirt. He quickly pulled on the shorts and shirt.

"I'm coming," he stated loudly, moving toward the door. He couldn't help grinning at Joan's giggles. He glanced over his shoulder, holding a finger to his lips.

As Mason reached the door, David spoke. "Don't let too much cold air in."

Mason shook his head and looked out the peephole. "It's the manager." He unlocked the door and cracked it open. Bright sunlight hit his eyes. Mason shielded them and peered around the opening.

"Sorry to bother you, folks." Wind whipped the man's hair back and forth.

"It's okay," Mason offered. "What's up?"

"Power went out around three a.m. and came back on a couple of hours ago. Hot water tanks are still heating water, so take it easy on using it. 'Shower with a friend and save water' is my wife's motto in these situations." The manager winked and continued. "Got a couple of messages for you. The airport remains closed due to blowing and drifting. Your employer also called and asked that you check in with them later today."

Mason thanked him and told him they would let him know if they needed to stay longer. Closing the door, he turned, finding Joan huddled under the blankets and David pulling on his sleep shorts.

"Damn, this floor is cold." David hopped around, pulling on the first two socks he found. "Where's my shirt?"

"Here," Joan began, tucking the blankets around her. "You can have this one." She moved under the blankets as though she tried to remove the shirt she wore.

"Hon, keep it on. I can find one real quick." David dashed into the closet and came out with a T-shirt on. Mason pointed at his feet. "Yes, I've got two mismatched socks on. How can you stand the cold floor?"

"Not very well. I thought I'd warm them up on Joan instead." Mason dashed toward the bed, grabbing the edge of the covers near him and tugged.

Giggles and laughter soon replaced Joan's squeals and breathy nos. David snuggled close to her backside, rubbing his hands up and down her back, egging her on to let him warm them up on her breasts. Mason grinned and slid his feet closer to her legs, whispering about warming them on her thighs. Joan sighed and settled back in David and Mason's embrace.

"What time is it anyway?" David tried to turn to see the bedside clock.

Mason chuckled. "Rather than twist your neck in knots and let cool air under the blankets. Just look at my watch." Mason stuck his arm in front of David.

"Damn. Eleven a.m. We'd still be asleep if he hadn't knocked." David inched his hands close to Joan's breasts, working his shirt higher as he went.

Joan smacked at his hand and squirmed closer to Mason. "Behave yourself. Both of you."

"Why behave?" Mason sat up and grabbed the edge of the blanket wrapped around Joan. "I loved our misbehaving last night. How's about more?"

David coughed and snorted. "Requesting a repeat performance already? Damn, dude, been that long since you got laid?"

Mason looked down and kept quiet. He wrung his hands and sighed.

Joan scrambled out from under the blankets and scooted across the bed. "David, I hope you're kidding." She touched Mason's arm and reached toward his face.

Mason raised his head, a goofy smile curling his lips. "Since a hot session like last night, you bet! Who wouldn't want to repeat that?"

David shook his head. "I agree. Can we discuss this after we eat and shower?" His stomach growled loudly.

Joan cuffed David on the arm and turned back to Mason. "You and your quirky sense of humor." She shook her finger at him. "It's a good thing I love you as much as I do."

"What about me?" David pouted his lip and looked forlorn as Joan glanced at him.

Smirking, she patted his cheek. "You are loved, too. Now who's showering first? That water is bound to be a bit cold."

Mason inhaled sharply as Joan told David she loved him. He wondered what she meant by it as she told each of them. Did she love them the same? Differently? As a friend? His mind raced forward coming up with question after question and growing rejected feelings. There were still a lot of unknowns. David was right; food and clean clothes offered a unique perspective on things that, combined with coffee, might clear the way for more discussion and clarity.

"I'll go first if David will make the coffee. He's better at it than me for sure unless you like yours thick, dark, and burnt." Mason grinned and stripped off his shirt. "I won't be long if the water is that cold. Certainly will wake me up for sure. But clean and dry is better than musky and hot—wait, there is a time and place for the latter, right?" He trotted past Joan, pinching her ass and winking at her.

David chuckled. "I'll make the coffee. Joan, can you see what we have for breakfast food? I'll let you go next on the shower. By then, maybe the water will have gotten to mildly warm."

Joan stuck her tongue out at him. "I'm showering with Mason to save water. You can join me to save water when he's done. I suspect we'll need to rush, so don't be long."

Joan shucked David's shirt and tossed it at him. "Take care of this while you see what's available besides leftovers and coffee. Thanks." She trotted past David, staying close to Mason.

David caught the shirt and drew it taut in his hands. "Getting cocky with me?"

"Yep." Joan waved and shoved Mason in front of her.

"Wait. I said I'd go first to a cold shower. That's all." Mason threw up his hands and skittered away from David, darting into the bathroom. Mason called out as he started to close the door. "Joan, if you're sharing, get in here, cuz once I shut the door you're on your own."

"Hey, I'll wash your back," Joan offered, hastily following Mason into the bathroom.

David chuckled as the door clicked shut. Joan might not get off as easily as she thought. Mason's wicked sense of humor...

"Damn, that's cold!" Joan's shriek, muffled by the door, reached David. His smile grew. Pointing his finger at the door, he mouthed "Got ya."

Joan tried to exit the shower as quickly as she had entered. "Mason, did you turn any hot water on?" She wrapped her arms around herself and tried to keep her teeth from chattering.

Mason cleared his throat. "I did. If you had waited a couple of moments, you wouldn't have gotten hit with the first blast coming out." He stepped in and pulled the curtain closed. "Come here, I'll warm you up."

Joan pushed her hair off her face and arched an eyebrow. "You honestly think I'm gonna trust—Ooh."

Mason pulled her to him and brushed his lips over her shoulder. Cupping her breasts, he thumbed her nipples. "How about I see if I can coax these smoldering coals into a fire?'

Joan gulped air as Mason nipped and suckled his way along her shoulder, working toward her neck. He slipped his hand down her hip and along her mons. Warmth started radiating in her belly, flowing upward toward her breasts.

"Please don't stop," Joan whispered, turning so her lips met his as Mason raised his head. She brushed her lips over his, pausing to rest her forehead against him. "If there were time to enjoy this fully, I'd bend over and let you take me right now."

Mason smiled and slid his hand between her legs while lifting her hand to his shoulder. "Steady yourself, and let me ease the heat some for you. We'll continue later. Okay?"

Joan nodded and parted her legs. She could feel her slickness from the previous night growing as Mason lightly fingered her clit. Gasping, Joan gripped his shoulder. "Work two fingers inside me and stroke my G-spot. That soft nub just a bit in. If you can rub your thumb over my clit, I'll—" Joan groaned.

Mason thrust his fingers in and out of her in short strokes, rubbing her clit on alternate strokes. Capturing her lips with his, he eased his tongue along her open mouth and inside, enjoying her taste and feel.

He didn't have to wait long for Joan to let him know how close she was. She broke off the kiss, panting. "I'm there...oh yes—hot and sweet."

Joan tossed her head back, arching her neck, pushing her breasts out. Her sensitive nipples grazed across Mason's chest, sending strong ripples of desire plunging into her. Threading her hand into Mason's hair, she fisted his hair in her hand and pressed her lips to his. Plunging her tongue into his mouth, she moaned her release as he began French kissing her.

Chapter Fourteen

David managed to pry his ear away from the door once he heard the shower curtain ripple along the pole. Damn, he loved hearing Joan's pleasure and knowing Mason enjoyed bringing her off. He wished he could join them. But coffee—drinkable coffee—and some form of breakfast needed to be started.

Rummaging amongst the cabinets, he located coffee cups and paper filters for the brewer. Fresh drip tasted better than instant. Since instant was the flavor of the day, he measured enough for three cups into the filter-lined basket and added water to the coffeemaker. Two containers sat next to the box of instant oatmeal, powdered creamer, and sugar. Joan knew how to eat quick and cheap. One last cabinet revealed their array of dry goods. Pop-Tarts and raisins completed the lineup. It wasn't a gourmet meal by any means, though nourishing and filling for the time being.

David looked up as the bathroom door clicked open. Mason waved him over. "There's some warm water coming out. Joan is washing her hair. I'm done. Get in and say good morning."

Mason's wink and grin said he'd enjoyed his shower with Joan. Now it was David's turn. "You bet. Coffee is done. Can you hold off on eating until we're done and out?"

"Yes, I'll get the table ready. Let me get my stuff out of the bathroom. I'll dress out here." Mason high-fived David as he passed. "I hope Joan's multi-orgasmic."

David chuckled and nodded. "Oh, yes. Very multi-orgasmic. Great, you two are comfortable with each other and enjoyed the shower so much."

David quickly shut the door behind him. Joan's humming greeted him as he entered the shower. "Which tune is that?"

Joan's eek and snort echoed.

"Damn it, David. Don't scare me." Joan turned and shook a finger at him. "Sneaking up on me isn't kosher."

David grabbed her and pulled her to him. Her breasts pushed against his chest. "Good morning, sweetie."

Joan tossed her head, easing her wet hair off her face. "Uhmm, morning, hon. You're acting different."

David stuck his hand under the running water. Its tepid temperature indicated he needed to get under it quickly. "Still waking up and dealing with a few jealousy bumps."

Joan cocked her head and stared at him for several moments. She opened her mouth to speak.

David held up a hand and spoke first. "No, I'm not jealous of Mason *per se*. I'm feeling out you and him being sexual where I can hear it but not see it. New emotion and experience. Now let me under that water, please."

Joan smiled and rose on her tiptoes. She brushed her lips against his. "I get it. I would feel the same probably if it were you and another gal." She inched by him, keeping her back against the inside wall.

"Are you done?" David slicked the soap across his chest and arms. "My back could use a good soaping, if you don't mind."

Joan caught his wink and returned it. "Sure. You can use my shampoo. It's right beside you."

David nodded and ducked his head under the spray. "Shit, that is growing cold fast. Hurry up, woman. Don't need to freeze my ass or balls off."

Joan giggled and slid her soapy hands down David's back, over his buttocks, reaching between his legs. "What about your cock? I'd think that was a bit more important than these." She cupped his balls and fondled them gently.

David hissed and grunted. "Keep it up, and I'm gonna bend you over the sink. Have my way with you while Mason listens."

"Hmmm, that sounds like fun." Joan slid her hand as far forward as she could and began rubbing her hand back and forth.

"Love to tempt fate? Keep it up, and you will find out what I've got in mind." David's husky tone and jerky hip movements told Joan he wanted to play. And, in the hot, sexual way like he'd described.

"Tempting if it gets me this." She pulled her hand back and slipped it around David's waist. Combing her fingers through his pubic hair, she circled his shaft and squeezed, slowly stroking upward.

"Damn, woman. That feels so–o–o good," David groaned. "Let me rinse and join you under the heat lamp."

Joan snickered and exited the shower. "Your towel is on the sink. Mason's is on the floor. Use it as a bathmat."

She bent over, wrapping one towel around her wet locks. Grabbing up another, she hastily dried off. The shower curtain rings pinged as they rolled along the pole. She picked up David's towel and turned.

His freshly washed hair stood up in places as he ran his hand through it working excess water out. His short red locks resembled mini horns sticking out all over his head. Unshaven, his beard line gave him an otherworldly look. Joan licked her lips and glanced lower.

Jutting out from his groin, David's hard-on seemed to thicken the more she gazed. She'd love to drop to her knees and bring him off. Feel and taste his hot jism flooding her mouth as she brought him to climax. Giving was as good as receiving, right? Joan tossed a towel at David.

"That ain't gonna save you. Shouldn't give me ammunition." David pulled the towel tight between his hands, let go of one end, and snapped his wrist. *Thwack.* Another echoed through the bathroom.

Joan's short grunts and "hey" greeted Mason as he cracked open the door. "Don't let me interrupt too much," he teased. "How much longer do you need?"

David reached out and pinched Joan's ass. She jumped and faced him. Shaking her breasts at him, she stepped forward.

"Give me about ten minutes." David started toward the door. Joan grabbed his hand, stopping him.

"I'll behave for a quickie." She winked, spun around, and bent over, resting her hands on the sink. "Come and get it."

She stuck out her tongue at David's reflection in the mirror. His hands slid down his chest, tweaking his nipples before moving lower. Two-thirds of the way down, he closed the space between them. Warm hands cupped her buttocks, caressing and fondling as David tightened up to her.

"Give me five to ten minutes, bro," David called out. "Can you check the weather for us?" Mason's hasty sigh and quick "yes" sounded as the door closed.

"Poor Mason," Joan crooned as David palmed her breasts. "I'd love to take you both on again."

David leaned forward, kissing her shoulder and nipped. "He got time alone. Now it's my turn. Believe me, you'll get us both again before the day's out."

Trailing his fingers in feathery touches, David traced the hollows of Joan's chest, dipping to her waist. Each time she dropped her head and arched her back, she moved tighter to him. Dragging his nails in zigzag patterns across her stomach, he lightly scratched and inched closer to her breasts and pebbling nipples. He rocked his hips forward, touching her, thrusting his shaft between her legs.

"Want me to stop and call in Mason?" David asked in between nips and licks on her neck.

Joan shivered. Leaning into David, she sighed. "No stopping or dropping. I need you now."

She covered his hand with hers. "Without a condom, I know we risk pregnancy. How about we play with each other? I'd love to watch you jack off while I take care of me."

David grasped her hips and turned Joan, rubbing his cock over each part of her that touched him. Lifting her, he sat her on the short counter area next to the sink. "Face me with your legs wide open, darlin'. I'm gonna taste you first. Dip my tongue deep in you and lap you closer to your desired goal."

Joan swallowed hard. Arching her shoulders, she closed her eyes and whispered her reply. "Yes."

She inhaled and exhaled twice before reaching for David. Joan leaned back on her hands and rocked her hips forward.

David kneeled. He slipped his arms under her legs and got closer. "Expose yourself, love. I'm gonna suckle you until you can't stand more."

Joan scooted to the edge of the counter. Placing her legs over David's shoulders, she reached down, parting her nether lips. She gasped as he blew on her clit. His hands held her fast, preventing her from moving more than a wiggle here and there.

David buried his face between her legs. His hot tongue laved up and over her taut pearl. Twice he grazed his teeth over her. She could feel herself swelling as he sucked her between his lips and began lapping.

"Al-lmos-st ther-eee," Joan groaned, threading her hands through David's hair and holding him to her. His tongue laved downward and swiped at her wet sheath. Rocking her hips back, Joan urged him on. "Oh, God, don't stop. A bit more and—"

David flicked his tongue deep into her and stroked. Joan's hands dropped from his head. She began shaking and moaning, begging him to not stop. Wave after wave of sweet wetness coated his tongue and lips. Pulling back, David returned to her clit. Carefully puckering his lips around her, he flicked his tongue a few more times until Joan eased back.

"No doubt about it. You are good at oral sex." Joan fanned herself. "What about you? Can I return the favor?"

David rose, grinning. He placed his hands on either side of Joan and puckered his lips.

Joan closed her eyes and pressed her lips to his. She reached for his hand, wanting him to bring her off again.

David pulled back. "Nope, you have to wait. Mason's been a good sport. You can play with yourself while I get off. But I'm not doing it for you."

Joan frowned and shook a finger at him. "*Now* you decide to play fair. Ha!"

David smiled and began stroking his cock. "Come on, love. You know how hot you get watching me pleasure myself." He fondled his balls with one hand. Wetting his lips, he put two fingers in his mouth, slowly drawing them in and out. He laved them from tip to his palm. He let

go of his balls and encircled the base of his cock. He stroked and squeezed as his wet hand covered the head. "Hmm, tight. Oh yes. Hot and tight."

Joan licked her lips as David worked several drops of pre-cum out and spread the residue around. Walking toward her, he worked both hands up and down his shaft. What did he want her to do? Play with herself to egg him on? Bring both of them off at the same time? Not an easy thing.

She reached down, easing two fingers across her clit. Even after two orgasms, she pulsed and throbbed with each stroke. Seeing David catch his reflection in the full-length mirror on the back wall, she stroked lower. Her previous wetness lubricated both fingers. She inserted them, locating her G-spot.

"Uh, yee-ss-ss," Joan panted. Her thumb hit her clit in counter rhythm to her thrusts. "David, I'm not sure how much I can—"

David's head tossed back. His neck arched as his hands stroked faster. "Oh, Mason, now I know—why—you love to waatcchh." Jisim spurted out and ran down, his hands dripping onto the floor.

David rose on his toes and cried out. "So damn good!"

Joan bit her lip to keep from yelling as her clit and G-spot began to pulse. Slipping her fingers out, she rubbed both over her clit in rapid short strokes. "Aahh, almost there. Can't quite make it. Help me, pleee-aasse," she panted.

David moved to her. "Yes, sweetie. You stroke, and I'll finger you." He eased his wetness-slicked fingers into Joan and quickly stroked her G-spot. Her muscles tightened. She closed her eyes and groaned deep in the back of her throat.

Joan grasped David's arm and fell against him. Her clit pulsed each time her G-spot throbbed. Ripple after ripple of muscle contorted around his fingers. He kept on until Joan's breathing slowed.

Chapter Fifteen

Mason stood outside the bathroom door. Too much quiet after what he could tell were two strong orgasms. He hesitated, wondering if knocking was a good idea. Still, curiosity got the better of him. He raised his fist and reached for the door. "Hey, you okay in there?"

David opened the door, his arm around Joan. "I think we're fine. Just blissed out."

"Want your robe?" David helped Joan sit down. She nodded and chafed her arms. "Turn the heat lamp off in there. We might need it later if things get cold out here."

Mason chuckled and retrieved her robe. Handing it to David, he leaned down and kissed Joan's cheek. "I think there's a bit of steam still rising off you. Maybe you need a cold shower?"

Joan swatted at him. Buttoning her robe, she rose. "I guess I need to finish up fixing breakfast. I'm hungry."

Mason offered her his arm. "Madam, I will assist you. Allow me."

Joan glanced sideways at David and then at Mason. "I'm too hungry to even attempt to guess what's going on. I need food and caffeine."

Mason took Joan's hand, tucking it in the crook of his arm. He patted her forearm as he led her to the counter. "Our cuisine is nutritious and filling. Not big on taste and variety. What shall I get you first? Oatmeal or Pop-Tarts?"

"Some of both, and toss a handful of raisins into the oats, please. I'm getting coffee while the getting's good."

Twenty minutes later, David put a second pot of coffee to brew. "Who wants more food with their coffee?"

Mason rose, picking up their dishes. "I'm full for now. I really enjoyed this meal. Quiet usually sets me off." He looked from Joan to David. "Your companionship filled the void I'd been using the television or radio to negate."

Mason started washing their few dishes as he continued speaking. "I don't want to go back to using noise to keep me company. I like having you around."

Joan stood, stretching. "Yeah, these last few hours have been like old times but with added benefits. Is that where we want this to go?"

Mason rinsed the last dish and carefully set it on the counter. Facing David, Mason watched his face. Would his facial features reveal where he stood on this?

David picked up a towel and began drying dishes. "I'd like to know how we each see this working out. It isn't a decision any one of us makes alone."

Mason set clean cups on the table and filled them with coffee. "I know I'm guilty of not speaking up before. So let me go first now. Okay?"

Joan held up her hand. "Fine by me, but shouldn't we check in with work and see what's happening with the weather?"

Mason shrugged. "I looked out the window and checked the local report. Whiteout conditions prevail due to high winds. Most of the snow has stopped. No one is going much of anywhere for another day or two."

David sat down opposite Mason. "I can try to reach the main switchboard. Last time any of us tried, the lines weren't going through. Our cells are charged."

Mason tapped the table. "I think we try to get through before we begin talking and let them know we're still stranded. We'll call them as soon as we know we can get out."

Joan nodded. "I agree. Try the hotel line. They got through to the office. Maybe we can get out."

David spent the next few moments trying several different numbers for the main switchboard. Ready to give up, he got through. "Hey, Stewart. Glad to hear a friendly voice. Joan, Mason, and I are holed up in Spokane. Conditions aren't clearing up any time soon."

Joan leaned over and whispered to Mason as David kept talking to the shift manager on duty. "Stewart must live in his locker. The man seems to be around no matter what time of day it is."

Mason smirked and pressed his hand to her mouth. "Keep it down. No need for all of us to have to explain what's going on."

Joan kissed his palm and laved her tongue across it. "I'd rather misbehave."

Mason pulled his palm away, shaking his finger at her. "Stewart loves to gossip. Don't know why, but he does. So let's not give 'em fuel, okay?" Mason winked and brushed his lips over hers.

Joan smiled, nodding in agreement. She made a zippered motion over her lips and kept quiet as she sipped her coffee.

David talked for a few more moments before hanging up. "Stewart wanted to know where you were, as you heard. I told him at the same hotel. That way, unless someone tells him, he can only guess if we're in the same room and bed."

Mason burst out laughing. "The man has a mind dirtier and naughtier than we've been in the last twenty-four hours. He's probably enhancing the story and looking for who he can tell first."

David grinned. "Well, you heard me tell him that until the airport opened here and roads were passable to not expect us. He wanted to put us on the standby schedule."

Mason sighed. "I hate working that rotation. I'm on it, and it's hell. No set hours or days. Let's get back to us."

Joan chimed in. "Work is a four-lettered word that we know awaits us." She pointed toward the door. "Out there, work talk is okay. For now, in here, it's us and where we go from here."

David stood. "I think, Mason, you brought up a good point earlier. Have any of us really said what our thoughts are? Spoken about what we'd like to have happen versus what can be going on?"

"I'll second that." Mason rose, taking his cup to the sink. "Somewhere between all the changes in our work schedules, we lost touch with our special connection. I didn't speak up and ask questions."

David placed his and Joan's cups on the counter. "I remember asking you if you minded me dating Joan. We talked briefly before your first midnight shift. After that, you've been aloof."

Joan turned her chair, enabling her to see both. "We've got to the point where the disconnect might have begun. Our mutual chemistry is obvious. Does why the disconnection happened matter? Or is how more important?"

Mason rinsed and dried his hands. "I suspect that both are tied to my experiences and squicks. You know things that bother me. I don't want to hurt the people I love and care about. You two rank highly on my list of those folks."

David moved up behind Mason. Placing his hand on Mason's shoulder, he spoke. "You know I'll share Joan. You've experienced it. Joan's voiced her feelings and maybe some of her concerns."

"David knows some of what I've thought about. I wished you'd come to me about your fears sooner. I'm guilty of not making time to talk to you about my feelings as well." Joan stood, dusting the front of her robe off. "Are you comfortable with where things are now?"

She moved to Mason's side, slipping an arm around his waist, and hugged him to her. "I want to know your answer regardless. Because what matters to me is that you trust me to tell me what is going on in here as well as here." Joan rubbed his heart and touched his head.

David walked over to the bed and sat down. "Somewhere in all of this is what's next. Can we drop our guards more and talk about that?"

Mason snuggled Joan to him. He turned her and pulled her back against him, sliding his arms around her. "I suspect we're not going to get everything hashed out. To answer your question, Joan, I've trusted you all along. I didn't know how to broach the topic or what I wanted until the last few months."

Joan reached up and patted his cheek. She tipped her head back until her gaze met his. "Understandable, and thank you for sharing. We're in new territory for sure."

David cleared his throat, drawing Mason and Joan's quizzical looks. "I wanted to make sure I had both of your attention for what I'm about to say."

Mason nodded and kissed the top of Joan's head. She squirmed and wiggled her fanny. David patted the bed next to him. "Why don't we all get comfy? No offense, Mason, but Joan's mind is in our pants. We can't return the favor since she is pantless."

Joan stuck her tongue out at David and plopped down next to him. "How comfy can we get?" She shot Mason a wink and turned to David, giving him a cheesy grin.

"You can get naked if you like. Just no starting anything until we've talked some more." David arched his eyebrow, hoping he looked stern.

Joan sighed and scooted back on the bed. "Okay, what's so important?"

Mason chuckled. "Honestly, Joan, you'd think we'd sworn no more sex. I think David is trying to keep us focused on making sense of where we're headed once we're out of here."

David moved up the bed until he was next to Joan. "Hon, unless we want this to end up a one-time thing, we need to gauge where each of us is willing to go next."

Mason sat on the foot of the bed, turning so he could stretch his legs out in front of him. "Let me state where I'd like to see this go."

He paused, looking at Joan and David. Their eyes met his. "I want more time like this. We're talking and sharing. I've missed this part of us. I want to date Joan one on one and share time together as well. And keep the three of us going strong."

David nodded. "I agree. Maybe we were headed in this direction before. Lord knows our puppy piles got touchy-feely a few times. Joan, what you think?" David hissed. "And keep those cold hands where I can see them!"

Joan did her best Cheshire cat grin and shrugged. "I'm cold. How about letting me under the covers?"

"If that will keep your two cakes of ice off me, you're on." Mason jumped off the bed as she reached for him. "I say we wrap her up in the blankets and snuggle her between us. With us on top of the covers."

"Damn good idea." David rolled off the bed and stood. He grabbed one end of the blanket near the foot and motioned to Mason. "You grab the other. And we'll tuck her in."

Joan tried to scramble toward the foot of the bed. Mason blocked her move as he tossed the blanket toward her. "Foul. Foul. Not nice guys." Her last words came out muffled as the blanket covered her.

David kneeled on the bed and tossed his portion over her. "You can come out till your neck is exposed. Those blasted cold hands of yours stay under there until they warm up and not on us."

Joan's fussing and cussing could be heard through the covers. "Come on, guys, help a gal out. Get me out of here, please. These things are hot and itchy."

"Sorry, sweetie, grabbed the wool one." David pulled the blanket back, exposing Joan's head and neck. "You wanted to get warm."

"Yes, but not alone." Joan thrust her arms out and fanned herself. Mason plopped down next to her. David smiled as Mason kissed Joan's cheek.

"Given our schedules, we don't get much time together. This is going to need priority if we're going to get over some bumps and lumps along the way." David dropped down on the bed and scooted over next to Joan.

"I agree," Mason said, pulling more of the blanket off Joan. "I'm willing to set aside a night or two when I'm off. Even make sure our schedules are available to each of us."

"Logistics are good. I'm curious about a word we've used." Joan grasped David's hand. "I know you love me. We've talked about how it's grown from friends into lovers with the potential for more."

She reached for Mason's hand. "You and I said it differently. We've admitted we love each other."

Mason nodded.

"What I want to know is how do you define your feelings, Mason? A bit more concrete words are going to help me understand what we want to move forward on." Joan squeezed his hand.

Chapter Sixteen

"Love is an awkward concept to define in absolutes." Mason glanced at David, catching his nod of agreement. "Before now, I would have settled for friends with benefits, i.e., loving friends. After last night, I'm in love with you, Joan. I hope I don't have to give you up."

David let go of Joan's hand. He stretched out on the bed near Mason and Joan. "I know reassurance is something that will take time to set in. I'm going to say this in the best way I know how. Give me your hands."

Joan and Mason hesitated. David sat up and crossed his legs. He leaned forward, gesturing with his open hands. "Come on. Put your hand in mine."

Joan looked at Mason, shrugged, and edged closer to David. She turned sideways between them. Slipping her hand into David's, she offered Mason her other one. "Might as well join in."

Mason scooted closer to both of them. Wiping his hand on his shorts, he took Joan's hand and gripped David's. "I'm not sure what's next, but you got me." He smiled and raised their joined hands.

"Now, I am committing to there being an us. No matter what happens once we walk out of this room, we'll go on. Are you committing as well?"

Mason licked his lips and swallowed. Was he in or not? David couldn't put it any plainer. Joan knew he trusted her. Each of them had taken chances. Things might not work out.

Were there any certainties in life? Maybe not, but things were a hell of a lot better with friends and

love. When the friends became lovers and—hmmm, what did they call themselves? Time to settle that later. Yes, he was in. All the way in.

Mason squeezed Joan's hand and grinned. Turning to David, he winked. "Yes, I'm committing. All the way and wholeheartedly. Some unknowns ahead. I'm sure we'll come out the other side intact."

Joan smiled and returned Mason's squeeze. "I'm committing too. And leaping in, knowing you'll both catch me." She squeezed David's hand and leaned toward him. "Love you. Pass it on."

"Love you, too." David turned to Mason, winked and squeezed his hand. "I'm glad you're in. Don't worry about me jumping you. You ain't my type. But dude, I've loved ya for some time. Pass it on."

"Pass what on? That I ain't your type? Sheesh, I think Joan knows that already." Mason laughed.

"No silly," Joan burst out in between snickers. "Pass on the love."

Mason took a deep breath. He looked at David. A quick peek at Joan showed she watched him as intently as David did. "New territory, for sure. You aren't my type, either. Joan is for sure, though. I love you, too, man. I'm passing it on."

Mason leaned to Joan, blew her a kiss, and spoke. "I love you. Let's keep the energy flowing together and apart. In pairs and as three."

David leaned toward Joan. "Is the circle complete, or does it overlap?"

Joan turned to him. "I love you both." She smiled at Mason.

Mason smiled back and raised their joined hands. "Let it be known from this day forward we are family."

"Agreed," David called out.

I second," Joan said. Loosening her hand from David's, she covered her mouth, yawning.

"Stop that." Mason started yawning, too. "Lord, I don't know why I'm so tired."

David looked past Joan. "We've been talking for a couple of hours. Considering how late we were up last night, I'm not surprised. I could sleep ten more hours."

Joan stretched out on her stomach, propping her chin in her hands. "I wonder if a nap is a good idea. I'm so sleepy my eyes keep closing. Even with two cups of coffee, I'm having difficulty staying focused."

Mason edged off the bed and stood. He stretched and bent over. Joan gave her best wolf whistle.

Mason straightened back up. "Uh-huh. Too sleepy to stay awake to talk more. Awake enough to ogle my ass."

David snickered. "I forgot to tell you Joan can be a female sex hound. Not that that is bad, you know."

Mason sighed and folded his arms across his chest. In his best miffed-female voice, he said, "I'm not your plaything. I have feelings, too."

Joan clapped her hand over her mouth. Eeks and giggles spilled forth regardless. David stood and camped as he walked over to Mason, stopping as he reached Mason's side.

"Me, too, girlfriend. We're more than play toys or sex objects." David tried batting his eyes at Joan.

Joan rolled to her side, wrapping her arms around her waist. Tears began falling the harder she laughed. "Ooh—ohh, please stop," she gasped in between peals of laughter. "My sides hurt."

David trotted around the bed and grabbed her ankle. He started tickling her foot. Mason leaped on the bed, bouncing them together. He stuck his hand down the front of her robe.

"Say uncle, and we'll stop." Mason began working his free hand up and down her ribs, poking and tickling.

David looked up. "Don't make it easy on her. She lit the fire. Now let's see if she's game to put it out."

"Fire," Joan gasped, gulping in air. "What fire?"

"This one." Mason slid his hand down her hip, pausing to lightly smack her ass. "And the one burning here." He combed his fingers through her pubic hair, nestling them between her legs.

"Oh, yeah," David offered. "I can feel the heat of this one, too." He trailed his fingers up her calf, circling her knee and walked them up tight to her vulva. "Need some help, Mason, banking that fire?"

Joan squirmed, spreading her legs wider. Mason traced the edge of her nether lips until he encountered wetness. David's hand brushed his. "Help is welcomed. I think this is a two-alarm fire. Needs two men to put it out."

David caressed the cleft of her ass cheeks, moving higher until his fingers stroked opposite Mason's. "I agree. You take the top half, and I'll work the bottom. We'll meet somewhere in the middle."

Mason worked his way backward until he reached Joan's waist. Removing his hand from between her legs, he turned sideways and stretched out beside Joan. He cupped one breast. Grazing his thumb across her tight nipple, he worked the cloth of her robe back and forth over it.

Joan groaned, rocking her hips from side to side. "I'm boiling."

David eased his other hand between her legs, working her nether lips apart. Near her clit, two large wet patches stood out. David leaned closer and blew.

David sprawled amid her spread legs and lapped. He blew up and down her exposed flesh, ensuring no part missed his hot breath. "Let's ramp the heat up more, darlin'."

"Oh—my—God," Joan groaned. She clenched and unclenched her hands. Mason's warm breath feathered up her neck and across her chin.

Opening her eyes, she saw his amused grin. "Hot in there?" he asked, plucking at her robe's collar.

Joan opened her mouth. Mason slipped his finger in as she tried to speak. "Ssh-hh," he began. "Feel. Nods and moans."

Joan inhaled and moaned, "Yess."

Mason's smile grew. "Let's see what's under here." He fingered the button closest to him. "Gonna help me?"

Joan reached up and pushed Mason's hands aside. She undid two before Mason's hand covered hers. "I appreciate the eagerness. Now let me enjoy unwrapping the surprise."

Joan giggled. "See–een it," she panted, bunching material in her hand.

"David getting to you?" Mason worked his hand beneath the material. He found what he sought. Joan's nipple pebbled harder under his rubbing palm.

Joan rolled her head from side to side. Moans grew in pitch and fervor as he stroked. Mason glanced over his shoulder. David's gaze met his.

David motioned with his hand, indicating they change places. Mason nodded. He brushed his lips over Joan's cheek and whispered, "Time to slip deep inside you."

David patted Joan's leg as he rose up on one elbow. "For sure, darlin'. I want to feel those hot lips and eager tongue-lapping me into bliss."

David worked his way to the edge of the bed. He stood and stretched. "Mason, I'll get you a condom if you'll finish undressing Joan."

"Deal," Mason stated over his shoulder. "Shall we strip for her or her strip us?"

David snorted at Mason's screwy smirk before he turned back to Joan.

"Eh, us for her. Faster and easier." David hooked his thumbs in the waistband of his shorts.

"Hey, I can't see, so nothing better be bared," Joan quipped, raising her head.

"Oh, now you're calling directions," David challenged, walking to the table. He retrieved a condom from the open box and returned to bed.

Tapping Mason's shoulder, David leaned over Joan. "I think it's not nice to talk with your mouth full. That is if you want it full of this." He shoved his shorts down on one side. His cock popped out, hard and erect.

Joan rubbed her lips together. Having Mason and David focusing on her, pleasuring her together was good. Last night they'd worked together to bring pleasure and bliss to all. Her internal temperature went up several degrees every time she thought about watching Mason jack off. David had reacted to her reaction. She'd gotten turned on watching Mason. She wondered how much David had been affected. How did Mason like being the exhibitionist and David the voyeur? David hinted at Mason's voyeur side several months back. If Mason's hard-on was any indicator, he'd enjoyed the view last night, too.

"Oh, your cock is beautiful," Joan murmured and leaned toward David. "I think the poor mindless darling needs a kiss."

David rocked back and forth, teasing Joan each time he got close to her. "Might need some cooling down, too."

Mason snorted. "Heat seems to be catching." He pulled Joan's hand to his crotch. "I could use some attention."

Joan softly fondled Mason through his shorts while she reached for David. "Got a question for you both."

David stopped mid-rock, allowing her to grasp him. Fondling both, she glanced at each. Joan inhaled and popped the question. "How turned are you watching each other? Male-male sex is a huge turn-on for women. I know you aren't bi, but it gets me hot thinking about you watching each other and digging it."

David looked from Joan to Mason. Another round of truth or dare? In the middle of having sex? Yet, Joan had a point. How much did watching and knowing the person fit into the mix?

"I'm not sure how much is a turn-on and how much is compersion." David smiled and shoved his shorts down his hips.

"Compersion?" Joan stroked him from his balls to the top of his cockhead, milking several pre-cum drops onto the tip. Rubbing her fingers over and around him, she covered his tip with the fluid.

Mason's low groan caught their attention. Joan smiled and eased her hand up the leg of his shorts. Cupping his balls, she held them.

"Compersion is basically that I'm happy and enjoy seeing you with Mason and being well-loved both emotionally and physically. That's my understanding of it." David thrust back and forth through Joan's hand, lubricating himself with his wetness.

Mason sighed and tugged at his shorts. "Got to get out of these. If my balls get much tighter, I'm gonna explode. Watching you touch David is one hell of a turn-on for me. As well as knowing he's enjoying it gets me hornier by the moment."

Joan raised her head and kissed Mason's leg. "Poor baby. You are a true voyeur at heart. I think you got a bit of exhibitionist in here, too." Joan grabbed one side of his shorts and pulled. The head of his cock peeked out over the waistband of his shorts.

David grunted as Joan squeezed on her stroke down toward his balls. "Easy, babe. Much more and I'm gonna blast all over. Not in your mouth as I want."

"Oh, no." Joan dropped her hand. "I want to taste you. So I'll stop."

David groaned and fondled his cock. "Damn, woman, don't let go so blasted fast. I almost fell forward."

Joan tittered and stuck out her tongue. "If your center of balance is that precarious, I hope you don't trip over your own two feet getting off the bed."

Chapter Seventeen

Mason tried to slide off the bed and pull off his shorts. His grunt and *oh fuck* got Joan and David's attention. "So much for getting these off and keeping Joan boiling."

He tossed the condom packet on the bed and placed both feet on the floor. As he stood, he glanced up. David's gaze swept over him as though he sized Mason up. Mason swallowed and grinned. "Now look, I'm not sure what's going through your head, but right now I say let's keep Joan steaming."

David laughed. "Not what you think, dude. I'm looking at how men can be so similar to each other, yet there are differences that turn a woman on that we don't see or notice. And besides, I like watching you two doing it."

Mason nodded, grinned, and shucked his shorts. "I know what you mean. I caught myself comparing us and wondering what Joan saw in you over me until we got together. Now I get what you're talking about. Guess we do look at women the same way."

Joan snorted and added her view. "Damn straight. Women do it to each other, too. Straight, bi, or lesbian, we size each other up if we think there is competition. Why still baffles me."

Mason tore open the condom packet and knelt between Joan's legs. "For now, sweetie, think about how you're going to keep us satisfied for the next ten minutes or so. I want to feel you coming all over me as you get me off."

David slipped his hands under Joan's shoulders and helped her sit up. "Raise your arms. I want you naked. If I dribble, I want that on you. Not your robe."

Mason straddled Joan's leg and leaned forward. "With help, we get back to the hot stuff much faster."

Joan lifted her arms, found herself sans robe and an itchy blanket. Rubbing her arms briskly, she looked from David to Mason. Both uniquely different and yet, they shared similar qualities. She loved each of them for diverse reasons.

"Now that's more like it," Mason whispered, running his hands over Joan as he moved back.

David licked his thumb and forefinger. Reaching over Joan's shoulder, he twisted and tweaked her nipple. "Copy my moves with your other one," he urged, leaning closer to her neck.

Joan mimicked David's movements. She wet her fingers and plucked her nipple in counter rhythm to him. She felt his breath rise along her jaw and up to her ear, adding heat to the growing fire deep between her legs. "Damn, this is hot. It's like watching myself in a mirror."

"Just feel. Don't think." Mason guided her free hand down her thigh and between her legs. "Stroke yourself while I get ready to bury myself deep in you."

Joan sighed, tossing her head back against David's stomach. His feather-light caresses along the sides of her neck and breast sent tingles up and down her belly. Each fondle brought new sensations to the surface. Her clit pulsed beneath her middle finger as she reached lower. A bit more and she found what she sought. Her pool of increasing wetness lubricated two-thirds of her finger. Pulling back, she circled clockwise around the edges of her clit. Not pressing too hard and yet enough to add her own bursts of heat to what Mason and David kindled. If she rubbed hard and fast on her budding clit as it swelled, she'd come. God, it would be hard and long. She

wanted it and needed it. Had she become like the guys? Thinking only about sex and the release it brought? Oh hell, why not? It felt good, and they weren't hurting anybody. "Hmmm, this is so good," Joan moaned. Leaning back tight against David, she slipped two fingers deep into herself. Thrusting them in and out, she moaned louder. "Ahhhh, I'm gonna come."

David caught her earlobe between his teeth and worried it. His hand cupped her breast and flicked his thumb rapidly over her taut nipple. Mason moved closer, raising her legs so her feet rested on his shoulders. Working the last of the condom over himself, he pressed forward.

"Ah, sweet heaven. That is so damn sweet," he moaned. "Tight and hot. I'm going deep, baby. No stopping now."

Mason thrust and pushed his way into Joan. "God, this position makes you so tight around me. Oh man, Joan. I can feel you flexing."

Joan smiled and wiggled. "What did you say, David, about a mouthful?" She puckered her lips, leaving them partway open.

David stopped stroking his cock and knelt on the bed. "Pillows behind your head will help with the angle." He cradled Joan's head as he eased another pillow under her.

"Well, now let's try it out." Joan reached for him. Her hand grazed his upper thigh. She trailed her fingers higher, working toward his balls.

"I'll make sure your mouth is full in a moment. Behave yourself until then." David picked up another pillow. "Mason, if you put this under her hips, I bet you can go even deeper."

Mason grinned and began pulling out. "That is one hell of an idea."

Joan tightened up on him. "Damn, Joan, you got a grip on me. Woman, you can flex for sure."

"You stay put and let David get that under me." Joan nodded toward the pillow. "Besides, when I raise up, you'll be deeper, too."

Mason groaned as Joan used his shoulders for leverage and lifted her hips. "I could stay in here all night."

David chuckled and placed the pillow under Joan. "I suspect Joan has a say in that. Her muscles might give out after a while. Effect of the position, you know?" He winked at Mason.

As Joan eased down onto the pillow, Mason massaged the backs of her calves. "Sweetie, I appreciate the flex and tightness. How about you wrap your legs around me and let me rock us to one hell of an O?"

Joan helped Mason ease one leg, then the other off his shoulders. "I'm ready to bring us all to that orgasm."

David knelt on the bed, positioning himself just short of her lips. "All right, madam, do your best. Worst is not what I'm expecting."

Joan gave him a raspberry and slurped his tip into her mouth.

"That is fii–nne," David panted. "Now cup my balls and suck me."

Joan tightened her lips on both ends and began bobbing her head. Mason's thrusts hit her G-spot, rubbing it in sync with her licks and sucks on David.

Mason inched closer with each thrust. Soon he was tight to her, barely pulling out before sliding back in until his balls slapped against her ass. His fingers tweaked and twisted one nipple while the other stroked her clit, increasing the friction and building heat deep inside her.

David threaded his hands through her hair and held her head. "I'm too close to blowing. Mason, can you—"

Mason's low-throated groan grew in intensity. "I–I caa–nn come now."

David picked up speed on his thrust in and out of Joan's mouth. "Tighten up once more, hon. And rub the spot under my balls a bit harder."

Mason kept moving, caressing Joan's clit as he watched David's face and movements. Watching and participating brought things to a new level. Exhibitionist and voyeur at the same time. Well worth repeating.

Joan tightened around him and flooded him with wetness. Her short breaths in between deep-throating David told Mason she'd hit at least one orgasm.

"Me, too," David yelped and let go of Joan. His ragged breathing echoed off the wall closest to them.

David slowly pulled out of Joan's mouth and dropped back on his knees. "Damn, I came harder than last night. That wrung me out."

Mason grunted as he slipped out of Joan, catching the edge of the condom before it fell off. "Wow, that was intense."

Joan raised her hand, waved, and sighed. "What you both said. Now that nap sounds grand."

Mason rolled off the bed, tugging the covers with him. David rose to his hands and knees. "I'm with you. Joan, can you move to let us get the covers from under you?"

She raised her hips as high as she could. "Grab what you can. I'm about out for the count."

David used one hand to support her while he worked the covers back. "Let it down, sweetheart. Mason, you got that side?"

Mason yawned. "Yep. Toss me a pillow. I'm too tired to care which one."

Ten minutes later, quiet filled the room. Sleep claimed them once again. Sated and filled with love, they snuggled to each other.

Chapter Eighteen

A week later

Mason stepped off the plane onto the open staircase. He hated leaving a note for David and Joan, but his on-call schedule permitted him little time off. Losing three days due to the snowstorm hadn't helped his paycheck either. Two double shifts at overtime pay had made up for the lost wages. He hoped Joan and David understood. When the dispatcher called, he asked if Mason knew how to reach them since they were next on his list. David's cell phone had rung twice while Mason had dressed and tossed his things in his suitcase. He hadn't wanted to interrupt Joan and David's lovemaking as they showered. His call had come as he dried off from his shower.

Pulling his cell phone from his coat pocket, he dialed David's number.

"Well, about damn time you checked in," David scolded. His warm tone eased Mason's apprehension.

"Yeah, I know. Notes aren't the greatest form of communication. I'm in San Francisco at the airport. Where are you?"

"Not more than twenty yards behind you." Mason turned and caught David's wave. "Wait up, and we'll walk in together."

Mason nodded and ended the call. He stuffed his phone and hands in his coat pockets. Patches of snow remained in shaded places, and a few icicles dripped from tree branches. A stiff wind blew across the tarmac, bringing a chill with it. Mason turned up his collar as David reached him.

"Still damn cold if you ask me." David blew on his hands and chafed them. "When did you get back?"

"Just now. I pulled a double shift. On-call is not working out. I need regular hours." Mason grabbed his bag and walked toward the closest staircase.

"Joan and I were discussing the same thing. She's picking me up. Come back to her place and eat with us. We've been talking about the three of us since you left." David started up the staircase. Mason hung back, unsure he wanted to know what their discussion entailed. David turned as he reached the top of the stairs. "What's wrong?"

Mason's frown and hunched shoulders spoke what he wasn't saying verbally. His uneasiness indicated he'd been thinking about their three days together as well. Good, part of their discussions prior to his departure was on what they wanted going forward.

Opening the door, David waited for Mason to reach him before continuing.

Mason reached the stair below him and stopped. His hand rested on the railing. His other held his bag. David could make out the tight grip of each hand. He couldn't say much due to other coworkers nearby waiting for them to pass. Mason needed some assurance that things were all right. "Joan's got a pot of soup simmering, and she mentioned your homemade soda bread would go great with it. Care to join us for a homemade meal?"

Mason smiled and nodded. "Sure. I'm tired of heat-and-run meals. I need a change of clothes, though."

"Joan grabbed our laundry when we got back, so I'm sure yours is mixed in with ours. Come on. She's probably waiting for us out front." David stepped inside and pointed toward the coffee machine. "Grab us a couple of cups to go while I get my other uniform from my locker."

Fifteen minutes passed before Joan picked them up and they were free of airport traffic.

David refused to sit in the front seat with Joan. His excuse about needing to put his legs up didn't pass muster with Mason. What was David up to? Joan's smile and airborne kiss added further mystery to what was happening.

Mason sipped his coffee, glancing at David in the rearview mirror and then at Joan. David guzzled his coffee and smacked his lips. "Ah, caffeine at last. Decaf just doesn't cut it."

Joan smiled. "Yes, it can add fuel to the fire. Especially when the preparers are naked with their wonderful cocks showing."

Mason coughed, almost spitting his coffee on her. She reached over, patting his leg. "Take it easy. I take it David didn't say much."

"No. Considering the first time I saw him was on the tarmac after calling you." David handed Mason a napkin.

"Before you two get started with your offbeat humor, can I know what is happening?" Mason wondered if not knowing might be better than knowing. Part of their last discussions had centered on their growing feelings and what form it would take.

"Sure," Joan said, easing the car onto the freeway on-ramp. "David and I've been discussing us. Us, as in the three of us."

"Right, Joan and I began looking at what each of us wants. We didn't get far as she got called to work a two-day layover flight. I've been doing the San Francisco puddle-jumper route for the last three days." David leaned forward, resting his arm on the back of Mason's seat.

Mason swallowed more of his coffee. Turning so he could see David and Joan more easily, he noticed Joan's wink. Was that for him or David? Maybe both of them?

"Our exit is next. Do you need anything from your place before we settle in for the evening?" Joan slowed down, taking the exit leading toward the main street six blocks from their complex.

"Not if my laundry is at your place. Clean clothes and a shower are about it." Mason faced forward, wanting to know what expectations either were not voicing.

"I hear you on the shower and clothes. Mind if I share your shower?" Joan's offer caught him off-guard. He damn near spilled the remainder of his coffee on his pants as he removed the lid to catch the last few swallows.

"Uh—if David doesn't mind, sure. I guess." Mason gripped the passenger door handle and waited.

David's light laugh and pat on his shoulder didn't help. Maybe he'd better ask the question running through his mind before he went further. "So what are the rules?"

"Rules?" Joan's puzzled tone eased more of Mason's uneasiness.

"Yes. What's acceptable and what's not." Mason shrugged and waited for either of them to respond.

Joan parked the car in front of her place and faced David and him. David leaned on both seats.

"That is something we hadn't decided on since you weren't available." David nodded to Joan. "Joan is right in questioning the word rules. Are we wanting something that rigid?"

"I agree with David on this one. How about you, Mason?" Joan covered his hand with hers. "I suspect you want to know about boundaries and limits."

"It makes sense to me," Mason stated, looking at each of them.

"Suppose we decide there are none concerning the three of us. We work things out as they come up. Joan's as much your sweetie as she is mine and vice versa." David opened his door. "Let's continue this inside. I'm tired of being cooped up."

Joan led the way into her place. Mason brought up the rear, thinking about David's statement about Joan being their girlfriend. It was new and different. No possession or ownership between them. It was like they were on equal footing.

David kicked off his shoes as he hung up his coat. "Mason, I know you've not been in a place where sharing was an option before. Or even one where equity was feasible."

Joan cleared her throat and spoke. "I've got something to say."

"Go ahead, Joan," Mason said.

"Let's go back to where we left off at the hotel. The last thing we discussed was that no one felt left out." David watched her slide her arms around Mason's waist. She briefly hugged him before doing the same to David. "I've wanted to do that since you got in the car. Along with this." She kissed both of them quickly on the lips.

David smiled and grabbed Mason's arm. "I want us—" He pointed to each of them before continuing. "—to go on. No one feeling left out or unsure of where they stand. All right?"

Joan slid her arm around Mason's waist and snuggled close. He hesitated in returning her quick hug. She understood his reaction. It was time for her to speak up. "Mason, remember when you said you cared about me, possibly as much as David?"

"Yes."

"I'm fine with that. I want to be with you both. There will be times when I will want to be alone with you or David. We'll work that out. I want us to go on. Do you?" She touched Mason's chest. "What does your heart tell you?"

Joan linked her hand with David's. "I'd love to know my new family is here to stay. What about you guys?"

Mason watched Joan squeeze David's hand as she squeezed his. David's hand rested loosely on his shoulder. David had stated more than once his views on sharing Joan with him. In Spokane, they'd broken down several barriers between them. Each of them had risked voicing how they felt as part of their last sleepy discussion the night before he left.

Mason rubbed his lips together and licked them. It was his turn to say what he wanted along with how he felt. Looking at David and Joan again, Mason inhaled and gathered his thoughts. Each watched him intently, waiting to hear what he had to say.

"You've both given a thumbs-up to our family going on and working through things. I wish we knew with more certainty how everything will turn out. That's my uneasiness talking."

David gripped his shoulder. "I understand. Sometimes you've got to take the risk to see where the road leads you. Joan and I talked about the same thing this morning."

Joan smiled. "Way I see it is we've got more knowns than unknowns. I'm willing to take the chance with those odds."

Mason leaned over and kissed Joan. He didn't just brush his lips over hers lightly. He captured her bottom lip between his and sucked gently. Joan parted her lips and met his tongue with hers. She turned into his embrace and deepened their kiss.

Two weeks ago, he'd been feeling left out and at odds over desiring Joan. Even commenting to David about her being a hottie had seemed out of place. It had taken a freak

snowstorm to get them together to spark their frank discussions and act on their mutual desires. Here he was, frenching Joan in front of David with no qualms. It felt right and natural. Yes, he wanted their family to go on. He was sure they'd work things out along the way.

David whistled softly. "Fireworks already. Wooohoooo!"

Mason broke off the kiss, resting his forehead on Joan's. "Yes, even more to come. I'm in on our family."

Joan's muffled cheer soon lost volume as both men pulled her into their embrace.

EPILOGUE:

Six weeks later

Mason stood outside, waiting for the bank to open. Today they closed on the house. David and Joan would meet him at the closing after packing the last few items in Joan's car. The movers were en route to the house. Finding the house in Cascade Bay and their new jobs with a local small aviation firm had taken them all by surprise. Little known about merger talks between two regional airlines had helped cement their move.

None of this seemed possible at first. Each of them had believed the other wanted something different. Heated arguments and passionate make-up sex had left each of them better understanding themselves. They'd grown more cohesive the more they talked. No matter what, they were family.

Where they went from here used to be an unknown. Now he had the knowns he needed. Even their new friends in San Francisco had introduced them to others who lived their lifestyle choice. The local polyamory community had welcomed them with open arms. There was still much to learn and do. Together they'd get through it just as they had so far, three in love and a triad.

THE END

Don't miss out!

Visit the website below and you can sign up to receive emails whenever Solara Gordon publishes a new book. There's no charge and no obligation.

https://books2read.com/r/B-A-RAUJ-MVVMC

BOOKS 2 READ

Connecting independent readers to independent writers.

Did you love *For the Love of Three*? Then you should read *Three Hearts In Love*[1] by Solara Gordon!

When Jon Smithson and Drake Cranston show up, claiming to be her date for the evening, Tina Davidson begins wondering what

buried treasures she may uncover before the night's over.

Brought together by their friends' wedding turned elopement, the three find their mutual desire growing. Acting upon their desire and

attraction is going to do more than heat things up.

---

1. https://books2read.com/u/3nNkAR

2. https://books2read.com/u/3nNkAR

Can two hunks, one lady, plus nights of passionate lovemaking create a lifelong future together? Are they ready for three hearts in love?

Read more at https://solaragordon.com/.

Also by Solara Gordon

Cascade Bay
Love Reborn
Reunited By Choice
Love's Triple Play
Three Hearts In Love
For the Love of Three

Cauldron Falls
Believe In Love
A Christmas Reunion

Peyton Corners
Falling for You
Caught by Love's Slow Burn

Standalone

A Heart's Desire
To Love You Again
To Love You Again

Watch for more at https://solaragordon.com/.

About the Author

Solara loves and lives with her partner of 21 years in the Metro DC area. What started out as a bi-coastal romance soon settled on one coast.

A vivid imagination keeps her busy creating her next fascinating romance. She enjoys creating unique characters and watching their journeys unfold. "Love freely given multiplies and will return endlessly" is a key aspect of her stories. Add in alternative lifestyles and her love for the paranormal, and the uncommon becomes the norm in many of her stories.

Her day job in the financial services industry pays the bills while she pens her erotic tales.

Read more at https://solaragordon.com/.